HE'S A DUKE, BUT I LOVE HIM

HAPPILY EVER AFTER BOOK 4

ELLIE ST. CLAIR

CHAPTER 1

*O*h, blast.

Lady Olivia Jackson just barely kept the expletive from crossing her lips as she took in her mother, Lady Sutcliffe, grasping the large envelope between her long bony fingers.

"Mother," Olivia said with a nod as she entered the opulent drawing room, its rose walls, gilded ormolu Wedgwood chandelier and intricate roses carved and painted throughout portraying her mother's touch. Lady Sutcliffe adored redecorating, and had transformed the London manor into a garish, elaborate little girl's dollhouse brought to life. It suffocated Olivia, but any time she voiced her opinion to her mother, she was met with a harsh stare down her nose and a sniff, telling Olivia all she needed to know.

"Olivia," her mother said in greeting, while Olivia's sister, Helen, smiled at her from the settee in the corner of the room. Olivia had hardly noticed her, so quiet she was with her nose buried deep in the book in front of her.

"I just received the strangest correspondence," Lady Sutcliffe continued. "In actual fact, I did not receive it myself;

however it was delivered to our door. Jenkins was quite insistent that no one by this name lived here, but the delivery boy was not deterred. Have you ever heard the name P.J. Scott?"

Despite the fact she had never been one to hide a secret well, Olivia attempted to keep her expression light as she pushed down the alarm that rose from within.

"Ah, yes, actually, silly me," she said with a tinkling laugh that sounded forced even to her own ears. "It is a name I have been using for … correspondence."

Her mother raised her rather pointed eyebrows as her gaze focused on her eldest daughter.

"Correspondence with whom?"

"That is the point of the assumed name, Mother," said Olivia, "to keep the correspondence hidden."

"I am your mother, Olivia," Lady Sutcliffe responded. "You need not keep such secrets from me."

As her mother made to open the envelope, Olivia stepped forward, rather desperate as she panicked to determine how to stop her. She said the only thing she knew would keep her mother from opening the envelope and thus revealing its contents.

"It is simply a silly love note from a suitor, and he would wish to keep his thoughts for me alone," she said in a rush. "I'm sure he would be quite embarrassed should my mother read his words. Not that he writes anything that would be considered inappropriate, it is simply —"

"A suitor?" A smile crossed the usually tight, drawn face, and Olivia knew she had said the right thing. She had distracted her mother with enough information to keep her thoughts occupied. "I am thrilled, Olivia. Who is this mysterious man?"

"Umm it's … that is …"

Growing impatient, her mother picked up her letter

opener from her small writing desk, intricately carved with the roses she so adored.

"Lord Kenley!" The name burst out from Olivia's lips. Where in heaven's name did that come from? She had met the man once at a house party. They had slightly flirted, to no great significance, and she had seen him but once since then, from across the room at her friend's wedding. He was, to Olivia's thinking, too handsome. He knew to what extent he attracted young women and he used it to his advantage.

Sadly, Olivia realized she had thought of him likely because so few other men had given her much notice in the past few months. True, she was never without a dance partner and found many men to be friendly with her, but none had any serious interest in her for anything other than a flirt at the many social events she attended. At one time she had been highly sought after, particularly due to her rather large dowry, but not only did she push away men with her propensity to say anything that entered her mind, but she had refused a rather high number of suitors and proposals, and the men simply had stopped asking.

"Lord Kenley?" her mother murmured. "Well now, that is quite the news. He is an earl, is he not? His father a duke?"

"I believe so," she said with a shrug, feigning nonchalance.

"Olivia." The force of her mother's brilliant blue gaze, similar to her own yet with such an icy steel to it, bore into her. "This is a *very* good match for you. You must not muddle this particular courtship."

"Oh Mother, I do not believe anything shall come of it at all," Olivia attempted to dissuade her mother, and to prevent her from taking any action regarding this ridiculous lie she had so quickly concocted out of desperation.

"Then you must ensure something does come of it, Olivia," she said with a sniff. "You have been out now one season too many for a respectable young woman. Any more and you should be considered a spinster, and then no one will ever want you. Now, do hurry, we are expected for tea at Lady Branwood's by four. Come and prepare yourself, Helen."

With that, she threw the envelope down on the table and stormed out of the room. With a sympathetic glance her way, Helen, younger than Olivia by four years, followed in her wake. Helen was a sweet soul, but well under the thumb of their domineering mother.

While Olivia's mother had always been concerned about her prospects, they had intensified of late, likely because of Helen. Her sister had now been out a season herself, her parents deciding they could no longer wait for Olivia to be married in order for Helen to begin her own search for a husband. Olivia knew her mother still hoped that she should find a suitable match first, however. It seemed to be becoming more and more unlikely, and Olivia knew her mother despaired of having two daughters left unmarried.

She shouldn't have chosen the lie she did, but she knew her mother would not have relented, and it would have been far worse had she opened the package.

Olivia sighed as she picked up the envelope as well as the letter opener from her mother's writing desk, and sliced through the seal.

This had turned into an utter disaster. She had known better than to have the correspondence delivered to the house. She had always been so diligent in picking up and dropping it off to the Register's office herself, but with an engagement the evening prior that left her sleeping well into late morning and the tea planned for this afternoon, she had no time to leave the house. She had thought she would intercept the post before her mother saw it, but she had been too late.

She was eager to read the envelope's contents, however,

publish financial advice from a woman, and no man would ever read her words seriously. She must be grateful that she had, at the very least, the ability to continue writing her financial column, even if that meant under an assumed man's name.

She drew Rosalind away from the others to take a moment to fill her in on the latest developments.

"Are you sure this remains a good idea?" Rosalind asked her with some trepidation as they stood by the tall sash window overlooking the street below, away from the prying ears of their mothers and other ladies of their acquaintance.

Rosalind looked rather pretty that afternoon, her long light brown hair pulled back off her face and into a low chignon at the nape of her neck. She appreciated Olivia's work and admired her friend for not only her intelligence but her ambition; however, she would never have attempted anything such as this on her own.

"Perhaps you should leave this behind you for some time," said Rosalind, "and focus on other things."

"Other things," Olivia snorted. "I assume you mean finding a husband for myself? I have told you, Rosalind, I am not sure how I am supposed to find a man willing to marry me for more than my dowry, who I find sufferable in return."

"For a woman offering financial and investment advice to men across London and beyond, I believe you have the ability to solve the problem of finding yourself a decent husband," said Rosalind with a wry grin.

"I have tried," Olivia replied, jutting out her chin. "And I have not found who I am searching for. Perhaps such a man simply does not exist."

"Oh?" said Rosalind, raising an eyebrow. "And who exactly is it that you are searching so hard for, who you have not found in five years at the balls you have attended and parties that your mother has arranged?"

"Someone who will not care that his wife is a financial columnist, who will give me the utmost freedom to do whatever I choose, who will stay out of my affairs, and yet, is enjoyable to speak to day in and day out," said Olivia. "That is who I require."

"Hmm," Rosalind replied with a nod. "I can see your dilemma. Finding such a man could be quite impossible. You have high standards, Olivia."

"I do, indeed," she said, and smiled. "It's my father's fault, I suppose. If only I could find a man like him. One who is warm, friendly, who would love his children with all his heart, and who would allow his wife to chase her heart's desire, whatever that may be."

Olivia's parents had an arranged marriage, like so many were. As high strung and overbearing as her mother was, her father made up for it in his warmth and genuine love for his children. He cared not that he had only daughters, and encouraged them to do as they pleased. Olivia wished so desperately that she had the ability to follow in her father's footsteps. She enjoyed listening to him as he rambled on about running the estate, about the finances to be managed for the household, the debts and the repayments.

In turn, he had treated Olivia as he would a son, and she had been enthralled with his every word, as much as most young girls were with the latest fashions of the day. If only she was a man. Then she could not only take on his title and his holdings, but also live as she wished, doing what she wanted, when she pleased, without having to answer to anyone — to a mother or a husband, or to all that was expected of her by society.

"How did you begin on this latest scheme, anyway?" Rosalind asked.

"Scheme? You mean my writings for *The Register*?"

"Yes," replied Rosalind. "I hardly think it a natural

circumstance for a young woman to be providing financial advice through a journal to the English gentry."

"I wouldn't say it's unnatural, but it is rather unusual," conceded Olivia. "My father subscribes to *The Financial Register*, you see, and I saw an article one day from a reader bemoaning his current situation. I wrote back to the Register with a response to him. I didn't sign it, but it was published, with a comment at the bottom asking for the mysterious stranger to get in touch with him. I did, but of course not as myself, but an assumed identity. And so P.J. Scott was born. The initials are from my grandmothers' names, and then Scott is simply in silent spite to my mother, who bemoans the bit of Scottish blood that runs through our veins from her own grandfather."

"Well, I for one am proud of you, Olivia," said Rosalind with a sigh. "It certainly must add some excitement to your life."

Olivia smiled. "It's wonderful, Rosalind — powerful even. You do remember, however, that you must tell no one of this. It is our secret and it must stay that way."

"Of course," Rosalind said. "You can trust me. Now, are you ready for Lady Sybille's coming-out ball next week?"

"I suppose," said Olivia with a shrug. "As much as I am regarding the rest of them,"

"Oh, Olivia," said Rosalind. "You cannot think that way. You never know what's waiting for you if you pull your head out of your figures and take a good look around you!"

Lady Hester Montgomery chose that moment to join their conversation.

"Olivia, darling," she said with a smug grin. "Are you still trying to find yourself a husband? After how many seasons, do you suppose, is it time to move on and accept that your time has passed?"

"Oh, do shut up, Hester," Olivia said with a roll of her

eyes. "Why must you be such a witch at all times? You may not have as many seasons' experience as I do, however it is not as though you are a fresh daisy yourself on the marriage market."

Hester's lips rounded into an O as she looked down her nose at Olivia.

"That mouth of yours is becoming rather low bred, Olivia," she said. "I should watch what comes out of it if I were you."

As she flounced away, Rosalind looked wide-eyed at Olivia, who was nonchalantly sipping her tea as if nothing untoward had occurred.

"You must be careful with Hester, Olivia," she said. "She's a right nasty one."

"Don't I know it." Olivia narrowed her eyes. "Never fear, Ros. I can handle a girl like Hester. I shall never understand why she feels she should be able to say such things to whomever she wishes. I do not stand for such women."

Olivia looked around her now. Mothers and daughters sipping tea and eating pastries, as they discussed one another's affairs, carefully guarding their words. Olivia always spoke her mind, which seemed to get her into more trouble than she bargained for. This was why she enjoyed her hidden identity. Under her guise with the Register, she could say whatever she wanted — as a man — and not have to worry about what she wrote.

If only life itself were the same.

time I begin to look for a wife. Your sister is beautiful, and it seems to me her only flaw is that she has you for a brother."

Alastair laughed at that, pushing back a curl that had fallen over his forehead as he shook his head at his friend. "Perhaps," he said. "But should you ever do anything to hurt her, you know you would have to answer to me, in addition to my father. If you're prepared for that, I would suggest you speak with him before raising the hopes of my beautiful, yet young and innocent, sister."

"Understood. And how does the Duke fare these days?" asked Merryweather, as he poured more of his own drink and looked around the rapidly filling club.

"Fine, of course," said Alastair. "I swear the man will outlive us all. He enjoys spending his days commanding the estate as if he were the King himself, frightening my mother and sister, and declaring that I must take more of an interest in the responsibilities of the dukedom. That time will come, though hopefully not for many years, and in the meantime I will continue to enjoy my freedom."

"And all the women that come with it?" asked Merryweather, his eyebrows raised over his questioning brown eyes.

"Absolutely," said Alastair with a laugh. "*All* the women."

"Can you honestly tell me that no one female has caught your eye?"

Alastair thought of the widows he bedded. They were warm, fun, and lovely, but not serious and certainly a little too overeager. He thought of the society darlings that fawned over him and his future title. They were all quite young, innocent, and fell so quickly in line to what was expected of them that there was very little, if any, intrigue or excitement to be had. His mind stopped for a moment on one woman that *had* held his interest for more than a moment. Lady Olivia Jackson. She had been at a house party he had attended only a few months prior. He had flirted with her, yes, but had done so at the bequest of his friend, the Duke of Carrington, who was interested in Lady Olivia's own friend, Isabella.

At least, that was what he continued to tell himself. It certainly hadn't been a chore spending time with her. She was beautiful, though not in a conventional way. Her blonde hair was more the color of honey than sunlight, and her nose was slightly crooked under blue eyes a bit too wide. When he thought of her, however, he pictured her laughing, and when she smiled it seemed all of her features came into perfect proportion.

More than that, though, she was interesting. She said what was on her mind, whenever it entered her head. Her mother had nearly had an apoplexy a few times when Lady Olivia had mentioned aloud what she felt was happening behind closed doors or between certain members of their party.

Alastair, however, had been warned not to toy with a woman like Lady Olivia, and he certainly knew better than to give the daughter of an earl any reason to suspect he was after something serious. They had parted as acquaintances and nothing more.

"A certain woman on your mind, Kenley?" his friend asked him. Alastair realized he had been drumming his knuckles on the table, a bad habit he reverted to whenever his mind wandered from the subject at hand.

"Too many women," he responded, his green eyes gleaming. "If there was one, that would be well and good, but I'm not in the frame of mind to be with only one woman for the rest of my life."

"You know as well as I do that doesn't necessarily need to be the case."

"No," Alastair said with a shake of his head. "It doesn't

have to be, but then I should spend my life feeling guilt for my pleasure, and that is not the way I wish to take it."

"Fair enough," said Merryweather, "although at some point you will need an heir."

"Someday," responded Alastair, "but not today."

* * *

THEY WERE MIDWAY through their meal when a bit of a commotion at the entrance to the club caught Alastair's attention. He looked up, and his heart began to hammer a bit harder in his chest as he recognized his own footman at the door of the room, being kept from entering by the staff. Alastair stood, stepping away from the table to meet the man at the door.

"Albert!" He called as he the man approached. "What are you doing in here? Whatever is the matter?"

"Lord Kenley," the man managed to get out between puffs of air as the man at the door looked on in disapproval. "You must come at once."

"Whatever for?"

"It's your father," he said, "something is the matter. His chest ... his breathing ... you must come."

Without a backward glance at Merryweather, Alastair took off after the man, not caring about the stares that followed him out the door.

He rushed out of the white marble building on St. James's Street to the waiting carriage, his thoughts racing. There couldn't be anything seriously wrong with his father, could there? This must all be some mistake. His father was a healthy man. He walked the grounds at their country estate every day when in residence, he imbibed no more than most men did, and he never overindulged in meals. He was a strict disciplinarian in every way, including his own constitution.

He believed gluttony was a sin, and ensured the rest of his family knew it as well, as he'd always stare down his rather prominent nose at the rest of them if they took too many helpings at the dinner table.

The carriage made the short trek to his father's stately white-stuccoed London Mayfair home faster than ever before, and Alastair was out the door before the carriage had finished its roll to a stop. He vaulted out of the carriage to the house, realizing as he entered that he had left his coat at White's.

"Where is he?" he shouted at the butler, who pointed upstairs. Alastair took the stairs two to three at a time, as he raced to the Duke's bedchamber. He heard the soft cries of his mother and sister before he even entered the room. He found them gathered around his father, who lay back on his pillow, his normally ruddy face now ashen, near the color of the pillow he lay against. Alastair froze in the doorway, and looked to the physician who was standing at his father's side.

"Lord Kenley," the man inclined his head. "I am sorry to come upon you in such circumstances."

"What ... what has happened?" he managed.

"Your father suffered some sort of attack," the man replied. "It came on suddenly and he is still fighting, but breathing seems to be difficult. I believe it will not be long now."

"No," Alastair ground out, shaking his head and refusing to believe the man's words. He had seen his father only this morning, and he had been perfectly fine. "That cannot be true. You must do something."

"I could try bleeding him," the physician responded. "But in my experience with a person at this stage, that will only bring on death more quickly."

Alastair sank to his knees as he looked at the man who was so strong, so healthy, so commanding, with all of his life financial advice into action. She had little money of her own to spend, no more than a small allowance for frivolities. It hardly seemed fair when she had a more than generous dowry awaiting the husband who never seemed to be coming.

If only she were a man. Then she could come and go as she pleased, to the clubs and the bars and the gambling hells where she knew she would not just spend money, but win it. She had a way with numbers, and anyone who had ever played cards with her soon refused to again as she was near to unbeatable but for games of chance. She remembered the numbers and suits of the cards — they flowed through her head as they were dropped onto the card table. In games such as whist, she knew what had been thrown and what was to come. She knew what sequences were available, and what others were likely holding onto by the hands they played.

Why was it that a gentleman could throw away every last pound, while if she were ever caught stepping foot into such a place she would be ruined? It was so very unfair.

The more she thought of the possibilities of gambling, the more it stirred something inside of her. What fun it would be to truly possess the identity of another for just a night, to get a taste of what a man must feel. She knew she could never make her way into a gentlemen's club or a gambling hell. But there were private parties which women attended. Not typically young, unmarried ladies, however, but women. She realized what might happen if anyone found out, but perhaps it was worth the risk…

She jumped when the door to the library opened. It was the butler, Jenkins, advising that her presence was required in the drawing room immediately.

Her mother wanted to see her. Well, that should make this day more interesting. She walked through the expansive halls lined with portraits of her ancestors, the former earls and their families, many of whom had walked these very same corridors. What were their hopes and dreams? Their reasons to be? Was it simply to wander this house themselves, have more children and continue to populate the family line? It was very likely, at least for the women of the family.

She put aside her musings as she entered the drawing room, where her mother sat waiting for her among the overstuffed, impossibly uncomfortable furniture.

"Mother, whatever is on your head?" blurted Olivia, who came to a stop in astonishment as she took a step through the door.

"A hat," her mother bit out the words. "Lady Bramford was wearing one the other day and I simply had to have one myself. She said it was the very latest."

"You look like a peacock."

Her mother's face tightened, but she refused to allow Olivia to affect her composure.

"I did not call you here to discuss my attire," she said, showing no reaction other than a slight tick at the corner of her eye. Olivia wondered how her mother managed to keep the rest of her facial features from moving along with her lips.

"Olivia. You have been out for five seasons now. Five! It is well past the acceptable time for you to be married. Your father may allow you your girlish dreams of love and such, but it's high time you realized that's just what they are — foolish thoughts of a young girl, which you no longer are. I've been far too lenient with you. You will find a husband this season, and therefore allow your sister to do so as well."

Olivia had been rolling her eyes at her mother's words until she mentioned her sister, and a roil of guilt flowed through her. She knew it wasn't quite fair to Helen. It did not seem right that Helen should have to wait for Olivia to find a match before she would receive interest herself. But what was Olivia to do?

"That's all very well, Mother, but you cannot force me to marry."

"Can I not?"

"No," Olivia said, holding her head high and staring her mother in the eye. "Besides, no one wants me anymore, anyway."

Her mother's eyes narrowed. "We can change that. I'll speak to your father about increasing your dowry. That should bring the young lords running once again."

"You shall do no such thing," Olivia challenged back. "I refuse to marry a fortune hunter who will then set me aside for the rest of our days. Change the dowry all you like. I will not give into your wishes."

"We shall see about that, daughter," her mother said back, her eyes glinting with a new steel to them that caught Olivia off balance, and she whirled around and stormed out of the room, slamming the door behind her.

Olivia's mind raced back to her previous thoughts on the adventure that could await her if she stepped out of her world and into another. She could be found out — but did she care?

What was the worst that could happen — her reputation would be further ruined and she would remain a spinster forever? She knew that at some point, when her father passed, the title and the house would go into the hands of a relation, but her father would always ensure she was well cared for. If she was going to live a life alone ... why not live that life well?

She told Rosalind of her idea that afternoon. Not surprisingly, Rosalind was shocked, though her green eyes shone with unspoken excitement.

"I hardly know what to say, Olivia," she said as they sat in the parlor of her parents' home, "I know what I *should* say. I should tell you this is a foolish idea and you should never, ever consider it."

"And yet?"

"And yet it seems like quite an adventure, though a very scandalous one at that," said Rosalind with a sly grin and a bit of pink in her cheeks. "Nevertheless, it is dangerous, Olivia. I'm sure you shall run into men who will know who you are."

Olivia gave a curt nod of her head.

"Understood. That's why I'll be wearing a disguise. Oh, and I've sent a note to Billy to ask him to accompany me."

"Oh Olivia, do not do that to poor Mr. Elliot," said Rosalind, strain showing in her pretty features. "He's always had a weakness for you. You know he sees you as the sister he never had, and therefore will do anything for you, even when he knows it's a fool-brained idea."

"He will not do anything for me!" Olivia argued. "We've simply always had a similar sense of adventure."

Rosalind sighed. "You shall ruin the poor man."

Olivia thought on it for a moment and then responded, "You are absolutely right, Rosalind." Her friend smiled back at her, happy she had come to her senses so quickly. But her heart soon dropped as Olivia followed up with, "I shall just have to go without him then."

"Olivia..." Rosalind warned.

"I'll be going only for a couple of hours one evening. Simply to see how I would fare at the tables."

"I still do not understand how you plan to escape discovery."

"Through my disguise."

"Will you dress as a man?" asked Rosalind.

"No, although that is quite a good idea," she said, and Rosalind emitted a rather unladylike groan. "However, the venue I have in mind is equally welcoming to women as to men, though not to unmarried society ladies. I believe it will be much easier to look like one of the women who frequent such parties."

"A prostitute?" Rosalind looked at her in horror.

"No, Ros, not at a private party. Perhaps if I were going to another type of establishment, but that may be a bit much, even for me," responded Olivia with a smile at her. "Many women gamble at these parties, Rosalind, just not the women that you keep company with. I'll go as a gambling woman. I will slightly alter my appearance so no one will realize who I am."

Rosalind looked like she might be sick.

"I would go with you, simply to keep you out of trouble. But … "

"But you are betrothed to Lord Templeton, and I could never ask you to do something that might jeopardize your future," finished Olivia, though she wished Rosalind would let go of the man who seemed an incredible bore and far too self-assured. "No, Rosalind, I will do this myself. It will be quite fine, you shall see."

* * *

"AH BILLY!" Olivia welcomed the man who entered the parlor with a friendly embrace and a kiss on each cheek. She had sent word to him that he should call on her to discuss plans for the evening, and he had come rather quickly, much sooner than she had anticipated. It was lovely to see him, as they had always got on well. Despite the closeness of their families, her parents had never attempted to arrange a match between them, as her mother had set her sights higher than a second son for Olivia. That was very well, however, as they had never any feeling toward one another except a close friendship, and both had always wanted more than that in marriage. Though, she supposed, were there to come a time when neither had found the love they were looking for and they each required a spouse, well ... perhaps.

"What trouble are you looking to find today, Olivia?" he asked, sitting on the sofa and crossing one leg over the other, his deep-blue eyes looking at her from under his mop of tawny-brown hair.

They had known one another since they were young, as their families were neighbors in the country and their London townhomes not far from one another. They had found much mischief together as children, and neither had lost that spirit.

"I should like to go gambling," she said with a smile.

"Gambling? At a party?"

"I should like to play cards for more than simply fun and pastime, Billy," she said, standing impatiently. "You know how good I am. I would like to actually play, against true gamblers, for legitimate coin."

He looked at her uneasily, sitting up now from his nonchalant slouch and leaning toward her, elbows on knees. "Olivia, you know, I am not certain this is a good idea..." he started, but she interrupted him.

"Billy. It will be fine. I shan't go to a gambling hell. That was my original idea, you know. Is there anywhere else that might be suitable? I had thought perhaps one of the noble homes that has been opened to gamblers. I shall go in disguise so no one will know me. And before you say no, if you do not wish to provide me with any information as to where to go, I shall have to find such a place myself."

He looked heavenward as if asking for help before looking at her with a sigh.

"Fine," he said. "There is a permanent establishment in the home of Lady Atwood. There is supposed to be quite the crowd tonight."

"Lady Atwood?"

"Yes, her husband passed and she had always been somewhat of a gambler, so she decided to make further profits off it by becoming the bank herself."

"Interesting," said Olivia, her eyes gleaming. "Perhaps I have a future after all, should I never find a husband to suit me. Do you have directions to her house?"

"I shall take you there tonight," he said with resignation.

"No, Billy, I will go myself. I cannot ask you to do such a thing."

"Olivia, I refuse to allow you to go alone. I will accompany you or you will not go at all." He gave her a look that told her he would not be taking no for an answer on this particular subject.

"Fine," she said. "I shall fake a headache to allow myself time to prepare. I will meet you at the servant's entrance at ten. Oh, this will be such fun!"

William smiled at her excitement as he surrendered to her wishes, though he didn't seem quite as thrilled as he shook his head, opened the door, and took his leave.

* * *

"Ack!"

William jumped in the air, letting out a shout, as Olivia poked him in the back.

"Shhhh," she whispered. "You'll wake everyone with shouts like that!"

"Well, you gave me a fright, appearing as you did so

suddenly behind me," he responded, his hand at his chest as if to slow his racing heart. "What in the blazes are you wearing?"

She had tucked her recognizable golden-blonde hair up underneath a black wig, which she topped with a satin Mameluke turban, unlike anything she would ever truly wear. She felt nearly as silly as her mother with the wide ostrich feather hanging beside her face. She had gone down to the shops earlier that day to find a few pieces to wear tonight and had been quite pleased with what she had found. She had kept most of it hidden from the maid and the footman who accompanied her, as she did not trust them not to say anything to her mother.

Instead of the usual white or pastel gown she typically donned for an evening out, tonight she wore a dress of fine silk in a deep red. It was much lower cut than any dress worn by most respectable unmarried young ladies, revealing an ample amount of her bosom. She would often wear a tucker with such a dress for modesty, but not tonight.

William's eyes nearly fell out of his head, as he looked her up and down, from her satiny slippers to the feather bobbing on top of her head.

"You look … that is to say, you are…" Olivia smiled slyly as he couldn't seem to find the words.

"Perfect," she said. "It seems I have the desired effect. Now, no carriage for us tonight, as it will be recognizable. We shall have to hail a hackney."

He nodded, agreeing with her, and set out down the road to find one. It came quickly, and he gave the driver the address, which was not particularly far. Her heart raced with excitement as they seated themselves inside. It had been some time since she had done something so carefree and reckless, and she was exhilarated. She loved adventure, something that was in short supply in her life. And she really wasn't traveling far. She was still within the neighborhoods of London she typically frequented, though she did realize they were coming to the outskirts of what could be considered safe for a woman of her station.

She jiggled the small reticule holding her few coins in her lap as she leaned back against the squabs and looked out the window. She hadn't much to gamble with, but it would be a start. She had spent the afternoon studying the game of whist. She had, of course, played many times in the past, but never in a serious fashion, rather more to while away the hours at a party or such other gathering. This was with true players, for real money, and she couldn't wait.

CHAPTER 4

The hackney drew to a stop in front of the modest, yet elegant and brightly lit townhouse. Olivia wasn't the only guest arriving, as she saw other carriages and hackneys depositing their passengers at the front door. She stepped out of the carriage, with William close behind her.

"I'll keep you in my sights, Olivia," he said. "Should you need anything, I shan't be far."

"Thank you, Billy," she said with a warm smile. "I don't know whatever I would do without you. Now don't forget, tonight I am not Lady Olivia Jackson, but Mrs. Penelope Harris, widow of the late Bartholomew Harris, a well-to-do merchant. We lived in Bath and I am just new to London."

He looked at her with raised eyebrows. "Penelope and Bartholomew?"

"Yes," she said, tilting her chin. "You don't approve?"

"They sound rather stuffy."

"Well that's the point. They cannot be nobility or people would ask questions about who they are. I had to come up with an identity that was believable but still respectable."

He shook his head with mirth, and she didn't miss the

HE'S A DUKE, BUT I LOVE HIM

way his lips slightly curled at the corners as he looked down at her and gestured for her to make her way inside. She took a deep breath. Here we go, she thought.

She entered the front door, and was greeted by a woman who had taken a heavy hand to her face paint, perhaps in an attempt to capture some of the lost beauty of her youth.

"Good evening," the woman said with a wide grin, showing her slightly yellowed teeth. "I'm afraid you have me at a loss, Madam, for I cannot place your face."

"Mrs. Harris," Olivia responded with a smile at the woman, as she provided her assumed name. "And you must be Lady Atwood."

"I am," she said with a nod. "Do come inside. What is your game of choice?"

"Whist," she said affirmatively. It was the game most suited to her, a game of skill, not solely chance, for one who was more of a strategist than a risk taker. It was a game in which counting cards would also come in handy.

A footman appeared to lead her into the appropriate room, what looked to be a former study that had been converted into a gaming room. Its dark green walls with pillar-framed fireplace and mahogany bookshelves lent the room a comforting, masculine feel. Former Lord Atwoods stared down at her, and Olivia assumed Lady Atwood must have been allowed to maintain this residence when her husband passed. Olivia was served a glass of brandy, as requested. She had decided a strong drink would help to calm her nerves and excitement, but that would be it — she couldn't let herself get soused, as then where would her game be?

Olivia sat in one of the leather chairs as she waited for the betting to begin. The game of whist required four players, and she could only hope she was paired with someone skilled, or all could be lost.

She saw a few gentlemen of her acquaintance within the room, and was careful to keep her eyes down and avoid eye contact with them. Her disguise was fairly clever — she had even added a beauty mark above her lip and had slightly painted her face, but if someone took a close look at her, chances were still high she would be recognized.

Truth be told, though, she was more interested in the ladies of the room. She had heard of women who gambled, but had never truly seen the serious players, only women at the odd social engagement. The women here were certainly more carefree, most of them easy flirts with the men in the room. Olivia suspected that most of it was a play in order to put their opponents at ease.

The gathered men and women — certainly more men than women — began to take their places at the tables, and Olivia greeted two other gentlemen she fortunately did not recognize with an easy smile. The men — a baron and a merchant — introduced themselves, seemingly thrilled to have joined her. Good. She hoped they would think she was an easy mark.

"Now we await our fourth," said the dealer, as Olivia looked down at the coin in her reticule, hoping that at the very least she had enough to cover the buy in.

Olivia sensed a new presence at the table. "I'd better have more luck tonight," the man said, his voice a rich baritone, though tinged with slightly masked resentment. The silky voice made Olivia freeze in her chair. She knew that voice. She knew it all too well. It had flirted with her for a week-long house party, and remained in her thoughts, despite her efforts to push it away. She swallowed as she looked about her, her thoughts racing frantically as she kept from raising her face to the man, allowing him only the view of her dark wig and the turban she despised.

"Well, either way, you are in for a treat, Kenley," said the baron, "as the lovely Mrs. Harris has joined us this evening!"

"It's not Kenley anymore," he said, seemingly not affected at all by the woman sitting at the table. "It's Breckenridge. The Duke of Breckenridge."

Olivia couldn't help herself at that, her eyes snapping up as they rose to his face. She had nearly forgotten his father had passed. Her friend Isabella had mentioned it in passing some time ago, and she supposed the Duke had been in mourning since. Her crystal-blue eyes met his of soft green, which flared in recognition as he took her in. He said nothing, but let his gaze wander from the tip of the turban-topped dark wig, down her body to the slippers on her toes, letting his eyes rest for a moment on the bosom that spilled out of her tight red dress.

She realized she had been lying to herself over these past months. She couldn't deny the effect he had on her, from his golden-blond curls, well-chiseled cheekbones and the depths of his eyes, to the deep dimple she remembered imprinting his face when he smiled his mischievous grin. The smile was far from his face at the moment, however. His usual look of fun and humor had been replaced by lips set in a grim line, as dark shadows hung under his eyes. Her heart tugged as she longed to ask more about what had transpired since she had last seen him. Now, however, was not the time.

He cleared his throat, a sense of amusement washing over the face that moments ago had been drawn and closed off. "Mrs. — what did you say your name was?"

"Mrs. Harris," she said, her nose in the air, as if tempting him to call her bluff.

"Mrs. Harris," he said, taking her hand and raising her fingers to his lips, never once removing his eyes from her. "Charmed, I am sure. I'm not certain, however, that I recognize your face or your name. What is your first name — and your husband's?"

She cleared her throat. "Penelope," she said. "My husband was Bartholomew." She saw levity cross his face, but he simply raised an eyebrow at her and nodded. She smiled an icy grin in return and they both resumed their seats. The dealer set the bets, and Olivia breathed a sigh of relief as she realized she had brought more than enough. That had been her one concern — well, her *most* pressing concern — was what to do if the stakes were set too high.

"Now then," said the dealer, an aging gentleman with a heavy mustache and somber countenance. While the game had a much more serious tone than the usual card games she took part in, Olivia was pleased to have the chance to put her skills to use, not wasting them on the usual partners of young ladies of the *ton*. She would never be able to go back to playing with Hester and her tittering friends. As much as she enjoyed winning against them, it was no challenge at all.

"Shall we determine partners?" the dealer asked.

He held out the French deck of cards to the four of them, and they each chose a card. The two with the lowest cards would pair against the two with the highest. "The four of diamonds," said the first man, a Mr. Ambrose. The Baron, Lord Stafford, chose the seven of clubs. "King of diamonds," said the Duke. Olivia chose last. "The queen of Hearts," she said with a smile, looking over the card at her new partner, who now exchanged seats with Lord Stafford to sit across from her. He winked at her, and she felt warmth flood her from head to toes.

"Right then," said the dealer. "We shall begin. The game is rubber of whist. Winners will be determined by the best of three games."

He dealt them each 13 cards, face down. Olivia raised hers in a fan in front of her face, arranging them as she preferred, her eyes flicking over the cards to the Duke sitting across from her.

HE'S A DUKE, BUT I LOVE HIM

The dealer placed the last card remaining on the table in front of them, face up to show the trump suit — hearts.

"Mrs. Harris," he said a couple of times until Olivia finally jumped, realizing he was speaking to her, and she inwardly cursed — she must pay closer attention to the game and not focus on the Duke. "You play first."

In all of her preparations, there was one thing Olivia hadn't counted on, and that was the presence of Lord Kenley — or the Duke of Breckenridge, she remembered. She would have to become familiar to referring to him as such. He had more than caught her attention at the house party her friend Isabella held over a year ago. He was a well-known rogue, however, and she had vowed that their flirtations would remain just that — simply a way to have fun and pass the time. She would not let anything come of it. She had done all she could to dismiss him from her mind following the party. He was too charming, too good looking, with a lock curling down over his forehead in the most captivating way, his green eyes boring into her, and his perfectly tailored and selected clothes. And yet, he seemed to have lost the easy, carefree attitude that had followed him in all of their previous meetings.

She withdrew herself from her musings to throw down the four of clubs. Pay attention now, Olivia, she told herself sternly, as she watched the seven, eight, and Jack of clubs being thrown down, the trick being won by the Duke, who had played the highest card in the leading suit. The next round finished with a win by Olivia, who played a card from the trump suit, which always won out. Play continued on, and when they came to the twelfth trick, few cards remained as the game was tied. Olivia saw the concentration on the faces of all the men as they struggled to remember which cards had previously been played. For Olivia, however, it was an easy feat, as the suits and numbers of cards were clear in her mind.

Knowing which cards remained in the hands of the players, she easily won the twelfth hand, followed by the thirteenth.

With the final score tallied, she and the Duke were ahead, though primarily due to her winnings. He had not fared quite as well, and while signs to one another were prohibited, she looked at him with a grin on her face, and he nodded in return.

The betting increased for the second hand, which Olivia and the Duke won handily. She smiled as she collected her winnings and thanked their opponents. They were no longer as cheerful, and looked at her warily before Lord Stafford left the table abruptly.

Olivia rose from the table, eager to find another game to join, when a hand wrapped around her elbow, leading her away from the games and out of the room.

"A word?" came the familiar voice.

"No," she hissed back at the Duke. "I see an empty space at a table over there and I wish to play again."

"Another game will await you in due course," he insisted, and led her out to the hall, opening the nearby closed doors until he seemed satisfied with a room.

"In," he said, pointing inside.

"No," she responded, crossing her arms. "Duke you may be, you have no right to order me about."

"In, *Mrs. Harris*," he ground out, and with a huff she finally acquiesced, flouncing into the room in front of him, taking in the cheery parlor, warmed by the fire crackling in the hearth, and the comfortable sofas before them. She looked around in appreciation before turning to look at him. "Well, then, *Your Grace*," she said, "what would you like to speak about?"

CHAPTER 5

*A*lastair took in the woman standing in front of him and shook his head.

"Lady Olivia, what in the blazes do you think you're doing?"

"Gambling," she replied, as she seated herself on the mint-green upholstered sofa, crossing one foot over the other and leaning back nonchalantly. Her posture caused the bosom that was already straining at the fabric of her dress to shift up even further, and he had to turn and begin to pace the room to keep himself from staring at it.

The vixen had no idea what she was doing to him. Alastair knew she was an innocent, that much he had ascertained during last year's house party. But seeing her here, in that get-up, her normally blonde hair covered by the dark wig, the dress that hugged her generous curves … the coy smile on her lips was an invitation to him, one he found difficult to ignore. Do not indulge yourself, he said in his mind, and attempted to return his thoughts to the reason he had requested her presence away from the gamblers.

"First of all," he asked her, "what was that in there?"

"What do you mean?" she asked, her eyes wide and innocent.

"With the cards!" he exclaimed. "At first I thought it was beginner's luck, but it didn't take long for me to realize you were counting the cards. You knew what could be thrown and when. You knew down to the last card. How did you do it?"

"What do you mean, how did I do it?" she said, her face turning into a scowl. "I remembered the cards. It's how one plays whist. Are you accusing me of something, Lord Ken — Your Grace?"

"Did you have a system? Someone helping you?"

Her indignation seemed to rise as she did, as she strode over to him, bringing with her the scent of jasmine he suddenly remembered from the house party last year. "Excuse me?"

"You cannot have been working alone."

"Why ever not?"

"You mean to tell me you remembered 52 cards, over and over again."

"Yes."

"It is simply not possible."

They stood toe to toe, glaring at one another. As angry as he was at the fact she was most certainly lying to him, Alastair could hardly ignore the heat coming off her body, and he seemed to involuntarily twitch toward her.

"Whatever your story is," he said, dropping his arms to his side and turning away from her, "Those men will not believe it. They were whispering to one another already and making to speak with Lady Atwood about you. Perhaps it would be fine had you nothing to hide, but clearly you do, *Penelope Harris.* What a terrible name, wherever did you come up with it?"

She rolled her eyes. "Does it matter? I certainly couldn't

come here as Lady Olivia Jackson. Can you imagine what it would do to my mother should she find out where I am?"

He couldn't help a grin at that. He remembered her mother from the house party they had attended. She was quite the dragon — nothing at all like her spirited daughter. She had been intent on finding Olivia a husband, while Olivia seemed to be doing everything in her power to keep from finding a match.

"Your mother would have an apoplexy."

"That is exactly what I said," she responded. She circled around the table that now stood between them and came face to face with him again.

"I came tonight because, whether you believe it or not, I am good at card games, especially whist. And I just ... well, I was *bored*. I needed to have some fun, and I am tired of the balls and the parties and the stupid gatherings we have. Any man can come and have his fun, whether it be here or a gentlemen's club or even a gaming hell. And yet I can barely enter another lady's house to play some cards. It is unfair, and for tonight, I simply wanted to know what it would be like to be someone other than myself."

Her breath came fast after the impassioned speech that had burst forth from her. She seemed surprised herself that she had shared so much with him, and he shifted from one foot to the other as he tried to find the words to placate her without encouraging her behavior.

"Have your fun, Lady Olivia," he finally said, "but you must be careful."

"What do you mean?"

"When I said those men were fixed on speaking with Lady Atwood, they were going to her to make accusations against you, to have you removed from her home. Whether you are guilty or not, being that you are not actually Mrs.

Harris, you likely do not want questions raised about your identity."

Her eyes widened.

"But I didn't do anything wrong! Why should I be punished for simply being skilled at a game of cards?"

He shrugged his shoulders.

"Life is not fair, my lady. Surely you know that."

Something in his tone must have caught her attention, for she whipped her head around to look closely at him.

"My — Your Grace, I must apologize. I was sorry to hear of the loss of your father," she said, as her blue gaze stared up at him from beneath long eyelashes with honest emotion shining forth.

"Thank you," he said stoically, not quite meeting her eyes.

"What happened?" she asked softly, placing a hand on his arm. He nearly jumped from the unexpected, though not unwelcome, contact, but he swiftly stilled his body.

"His health failed him," he responded, his gaze now trained on the flames licking the grate of the hearth. "One moment, he was striding the grounds, commanding everyone as if he were the admiral of a fleet of navy ships, and the next he was on his deathbed."

He cleared his throat, not wanting to say anymore in the moment.

It had been months since his father's death, and Alastair still had not quite come to terms with his new place in life. He and his father had never gotten along well, but now that he had stepped into his father's role, Alastair was beginning to understand more of what made his father the man he was. His father had become duke at quite a young age, just into his teen years. The responsibility the role entailed had been a part of him for all of his formative years.

The strain his father had been under in the months prior to his death now also made more sense to Alastair. The first day following his mourning period, he had sat behind his father's desk to make some semblance of order out of the estate's ledgers, which were now ultimately his responsibility. He had to call the steward in to double check that he was reading the accounts correctly. He had been aghast to find that they were apparently quite deep into debt.

"How could this have happened?" he asked the man, who shrugged and cryptically said that expenses had become higher than any revenue they brought in. Alastair had poured over the ledgers for days, but had come up with nothing other than what the man said. It was the expenses that nagged at him, though. There were large sums of money borrowed against the estate by his father, yet no accounting for what he had taken the money for, and no one seemed inclined to provide any idea of where they had gone. Alastair had to find out — and fast. As it was, he was here at this makeshift club tonight to see if he couldn't win a quick pound or two. He was fortunate he had been partnered with Lady Olivia, for she had helped him win a good deal of it already.

"What do you say…" he began, "we play together for the rest of the night? You can win, certainly, but you must not win so handily or boastfully. I will stay with you, and advise if any shift in your countenance is required, and will keep you aware of the circumstances. I am much more familiar in such surroundings."

"Yes, I can tell," she said, with one polished eyebrow raised high. "Fine then. Only because I like you, Your Grace. You were a good friend to Isabella this past year, and I also appreciate a man who can tell me the truth of a matter." She nodded at him. "Shall we return?"

"Lead the way, Mrs. Harris."

He tried not to watch her as she walked out of the room ahead of him, he really did. But the swish of her skirts over the thick round of her backside was almost more than he could bear.

Stop Alastair, he told himself. She's not one to trifle with and you most certainly could not handle a wife at the moment, especially a wife like her — she was a spitfire, this one. He currently wanted to worry about nothing more than whether to drink brandy or whiskey, to play whist or hazard, and to decide which gaming hell to visit that particular evening. He was already responsible for his sister, his mother, and the Dukedom of Breckenridge.

He sighed as Lady Olivia called to him from the door. She was so alluring, it was hard to think straight when she was next to him. He had realized upon first meeting her that one would never know what to expect from the woman, but he certainly had not foreseen this. What was she thinking, dressing up as a harlot and coming to a gambling house such as this, albeit in the house of a lady? He shook his head and felt a smile creep into his cheeks for the first time in quite a long while, as he followed her to the door.

* * *

THEY PLAYED A FEW MORE GAMES, winning handily — although not too handily — before Lady Olivia excused herself, telling the other players that she must retire for the evening. Alastair himself rose and walked with her to the door, as he could feel sets of eyes trained on them.

"I must apologize," he said, as he looked down at her with a sheepish grin, his hands clasped behind his back. "I was entirely in the wrong. You did not have beginner's luck but do seem to have an aptitude for the game."

"It's not the game," she said with a shrug of her shoulders. "It's the cards — the memory of the cards."

"Even still," he said, shaking his head slightly, "most

people cannot remember the cards within their hand, alone which have been thrown."

"Perhaps we should do this another time," she said as her rosy lips turned up in a smile. Whether it was the change in her hair color or the dim light of the tallow candles in the hall, she looked like an entirely different woman in the moment, her blue eyes popping as she looked up him. He didn't know what came over him, but he leaned down and gave her a quick, innocent kiss on those plump lips of hers. He pulled back immediately, suddenly aware of their circumstance and who she really was.

"May I accompany you home?" he asked, seeing the red of her blush seeping up her cheeks to her hairline. "To assure your safety," he hastily added.

"No!" she said with force, before softening her tone. "I mean, no, thank you, Your Grace. I deeply appreciate it, but I have Billy."

"Billy?"

"Yes, a friend — Mr. William Elliot. He accompanied me here this evening."

The man seemingly appeared from nowhere, and began to escort Lady Olivia to her carriage. Alastair felt a twinge as he scowled at the well-dressed, good-looking Mr. Elliot, who nodded at him in turn. He was determined to ignore the ire that this man raised, and instead turned back toward the house.

"Goodbye, Your Grace," Olivia called out as she walked down the drive. "I hope your evening and your purse improve this night!"

He raised a hand in response, and returned to the card tables but unfortunately after she left, his luck seemed to have disappeared with her.

CHAPTER 6

It had been a week since her foray into a new world with another identity at Lady Atwood's house. It was strange, really — while nothing had actually changed, in the same breath it felt as if everything was different. For once, Olivia had taken the opportunity to do something that made her feel well and truly alive.

She opened the correspondence in front of her, pleased to find an envelope from the Duchess of Carrington — one of her greatest friends, formerly Miss Isabella Marriott. It was an invitation to a dinner party she and her husband were holding at their London home at the start of the season, and they requested her presence. Olivia was delighted. She had not been to their townhouse in the city and it had been some time since she had seen her friend, who was most often at their country home. She wondered who would be present at this dinner, her thoughts touching on Lord Kenley — no, she reminded herself, he was now the Duke of Breckenridge. The Duke was a close friend of Isabella's husband.

She wrote back swiftly, telling her friend she would be more than happy to attend. Unfortunately it also meant her mother would be along as her chaperone, which caused Olivia to groan aloud. Out five seasons and her mother still had to accompany her. At what point could a spinster attend such events without a chaperone, she wondered. She had never deemed to find out, but as she was near to reaching such status, she supposed she should look further into what that would mean for her. Shrugging her shoulders, she rose to find her mother, as well as the butler to send her response posthaste.

* * *

THE CARRINGTON'S London home on Queen Street was one that spoke of wealth through its subdued charm and elegance, not the garish display of her mother's home, Olivia noted as their carriage pulled up to the front of the columned townhouse.

"How quaint," her mother said with a sniff as they alighted, causing Olivia to roll her eyes at her back. Perhaps she should marry simply to be rid of her mother's constant presence at such events, Olivia thought.

As they walked through the arched entryway, Isabella came forward to greet them, holding Olivia in a tight embrace for a moment.

"It is wonderful to see you!" she exclaimed. "How I have missed you."

"And I you," answered Olivia, stepping back to look at her friend. "Marriage certainly agrees with you, Isabella. Why, you are positively glowing."

Isabella waved a hand at her and bade them enter, her husband standing to greet them as they entered the parlor where the dinner guests awaited.

"Lady Olivia," he said, his dark head bowing over her hand. "I am very pleased you are joining us this evening. I do not believe I have ever properly thanked you for your assistance in my affairs at the house party last year."

"Oh, it is I that would thank you, Your Grace," she responded. "It was the most thrill I've had in all my life!"

Her mother snorted as she walked by them, hearing Olivia's words. She had found the entire affair quite sordid, of course, however she never knew the entire story behind all that had happened.

Isabella joined them then, her hand coming onto her husband's arm as she smiled up at him. How happy they looked, thought Olivia. Their love story had been one of adventure and intrigue, and she had been pleased to have taken part in it during a turbulent week at the home Isabella's parents had left to her upon their passing. While Olivia found the Duke to be a serious sort, she was rather fond of him. Above all, he made Isabella happier than one could ever imagine possible, and for that Olivia would always be grateful to him.

There had been one other person who was a part of their allegiance last year, who had helped the Duke in his quest — Alastair Finchley, who was now walking up to them, with a devilish look in his eyes and a mischievous smile on his lips. Her heart began to beat faster despite her best efforts to be unaffected by his presence.

"Ah, if it is not my co-conspirators all together, awaiting me!" he exclaimed as he greeted them. "Lady Olivia, I must tell you, I met a woman the other night who looked just like you, but for the color of her hair. A Mrs.…. oh drat, I have forgotten her name. Oh yes! Mrs. Harris."

"Mrs. Harris?" said Isabella with a look of confusion on her face while Olivia shifted from one foot to the other, the skirts of her mint green-silk dress shifting with her. "I don't believe I have ever heard of a Mrs. Harris, have you Olivia?"

Olivia concentrated on stamping down the heat rising in her cheeks.

"I have heard the woman is something of a card player," she said, "that is all I know."

"Yes, she won me a great deal of money as my whist partner at Lady Atwood's. You must all keep an eye out for her about town so that I can find her and properly thank her. She had hair the color of midnight, topped with a turban and a feather kissing the side of her cheek. She also had a rather fetching beauty mark, right here," he said, pointing to the place on Olivia's face where she had painted it on. "And her dress, well ... it was quite memorable, though certainly not one you would ever see at a place where the woman of the *ton* were in attendance."

Olivia cleared her throat as Bradley and Isabella looked back and forth from one of them to the other, obviously picking up on the subtle underlying tension simmering between them.

"Come, man, allow me to pour you a drink," said Bradley, leading Alastair away to where the full decanter stood with crystal glasses in front of it.

Isabella turned to Olivia

"Would I be so out of line," Isabella began, lowering her voice to ensure she would not be overheard, "to believe that this Mrs. Harris is none other than the same person as Lady Olivia Jackson?"

"You would be correct," she said, with a grin. She told Isabella the story of the late night escapade, and Isabella shook her head at her. "It's a wonder you did not get caught," she said. "And Alastair told no one?"

"He did not," said Olivia, "Although it looks as if he may be telling your husband at the moment, by the look of amusement he is sending my way. I do thank God he said nothing while at Lady Atwood's. In fact, he was actually rather helpful."

"If he had told anyone, I would never speak to him again," said Isabella, with conviction in her tone. "You are a daring one, Olivia. Are you still rather fond of our Alastair?"

"Fond of him? I was never fond of him, Isabella," she said. "Why would you think so?"

"I seem to recall a few comments regarding the man's backside."

"Oh, well yes, he certainly does have a nice one," said Olivia, stealing a look at the man who had now been joined by two young ladies, one she recognized as Lady Frances Davenport, a close friend of Lady Hester Montgomery. She was not quite as evil, but well under Hester's control. "Though I believe most women notice his backside, and if not, they certainly notice the front. His face, I mean!" she laughed at herself while Isabella shook her head.

"Yes, Alastair has his choice of women, it's true," she conceded. "But he did seem rather taken with you, and it seems he still might be. He has inherited his father's title and all its endowments, Olivia. He will be needing a wife in due course."

Olivia shook her head resolutely. The Duke was not the sort of man she would ever marry. "That wife," she said, "will not be me."

***

THE YOUNG LADIES currently batting their eyelids at him were comely enough, thought Alastair, though he had far preferred the company of Lady Olivia Jackson. She held nothing back, and it was rather refreshing instead of the sighs and tittering of the other young unmarried women present this evening.

He had not expected to see her again so soon, and he had been unable to get her off his mind, try as he might.

"Is there something of interest across the room?" murmured his friend Carrington in a low voice. "I certainly hope it is not my wife at whom you continue to steal glances."

"Steal glances? What am I, a schoolgirl?" he asked his friend with a laugh. "I am simply comparing Lady Olivia tonight to the woman she was in the disguise last week. Now that I see her without the wig and costume, I do realize how well she had disguised herself. It was the eyes, however. They gave her away."

Bradley nodded. "She's a handful, that one. 'Tis why she has been out so long without a husband. And the fact she continues to turn down all who ask for her hand. Apparently she feels none will suit her, and most have stopped asking to avoid the embarrassment. She seems somewhat taken with you, however, old chap. Have you a mind to pursue her?"

"Pursue her?" Alastair repeated with a laugh. "Certainly not. I am in no need of a wife."

"How could you not be?" asked Bradley. "You have inherited and are in charge of decently large estates. A wife would be of great help."

"Yes, but I enjoy my current life far too much. The cards, the drinks, the gambling," he said. "Already I feel guilty if I'm out carousing. What would I feel with a wife at home? I think not. Besides that, do you feel Lady Olivia would be one to sit quietly at home while her husband was about town? Certainly not."

Bradley shrugged. "Perhaps you would enjoy marriage more than you might think."

"Absolutely not," Alastair replied adamantly. "I promise you, Carrington, I shall be a bachelor for some time to come. Marriage, man, is not for me."

Bradley gave him a questionable look, but finally agreed. "Whatever you say, Carrington," he responded, and then set out to find his wife before they were called into dinner.

Alastair found himself seated beside none other than Lady Olivia, which he was rather pleased about, despite his conversation with Carrington. He may not have any inclination to marry the woman, but he would enjoy the time to have his flirtations with her. Though his intentions were somewhat dampened by the fact her mother sat down across from him and looked at him with the gleam in her eye that he had seen far too many times on the faces of mothers and daughters intent on securing him as a husband. He turned to her daughter instead.

"I have been remiss in telling you that you look lovely tonight, Lady Olivia," he said. "Your dress becomes you. Though perhaps not nearly as much as a red gown I saw you wear recently. There was something about it that was quite ... appealing."

She nearly choked on her wine as she stole a glance at her mother. "You must be mistaken, Your Grace," she said. "For it has been some time since I have worn red, it not being particularly in fashion at the moment."

"No, no I seem to recall it rather well," he said. "In fact, I cannot quite get it *out* of my head." He gave her a wolfish grin and lowered his voice. "Nor what it showcased."

He expected her to blush, or to look somewhat chastened. Instead, she laughed. He followed suit, until he caught her mother's look from across the table. The woman looked like a cat who had caught the mouse she had been chasing for days. He sobered, put a polite smile on his face, and turned to speak with Lady Frances Davenport on his right.

CHAPTER 7

Olivia swished the sky blue skirts around her ankles as she looked at herself in the ornate oval mirror that stood in the corner of her bedchamber. She was certainly *not* taking extra care of her appearance for anyone in particular, she told herself. Especially not the Duke of Breckenridge.

An image of the Duke came into her thoughts, but she pushed it away. The Duke was charming, handsome, and seemed to know the right words to say to make her feel a gravitation pull to him despite how much she tried to push it away.

It would never do for her to act on that attraction. If she allowed herself to feel anything for the Duke — whether it be sentiment or simply the pull of desire — it could turn into something very, very dangerous.

To fall for a man like the Duke would be a disaster. She knew that at least some of the gossip about him rang true. The Duke was a rogue, who loved women, and never one woman for any more than a short length of time. If she drew close to a man like him, he would break her heart, that was for certain. Besides, Olivia was too proud a woman to throw herself in among the innocent young debutantes who flung themselves toward him for his title, or the experienced ladies of the ton who wanted him for his charm and skills in the bedchamber. For while Olivia Jackson was relentless when she wanted something, she refused to share, particularly the affection of a man.

She reminded herself that she was not thinking of the Duke as she dressed that evening, or whether he may or may not be present at the coming-out ball of Lady Sybille, which would be held at the Argyll Rooms. It didn't matter in the slightest. All that mattered was that he kept her identity of Mrs. Harris secret. She knew she had made him a good amount of money through their games of whist that evening. Hopefully his gratefulness to her would be enough to still his tongue.

Her eyes drew upward to the artful style of her honey-blonde hair, pulled away from her face but for a few tendrils that drifted down her forehead to her cheeks. The blue dress brought out the color of her eyes, and its high waist allowed the soft folds of satin to fall delicately over her curves.

She smiled, straightened, and turned to join her mother downstairs.

* * *

As Lady Sutcliffe nattered at her all the way to the Argyll Rooms, Olivia was tempted to tell her about her visit to Lady Atwood's house just to make her stop talking, but she was too concerned of the tirade it would send her mother into. If she knew what Olivia had done, it was likely Olivia would never again have the ability to leave her room alone.

Instead, Olivia gazed out the window, turning away from the woman who somehow had birthed her. They were pulling up to the doors when Olivia finally turned to Lady Sutcliffe. "That's enough, Mother," she said, attempting to suppress the scorn she felt at her mother's words. Yes, it had been five seasons since she came out. Yes, she had turned away an ample number of men who had originally shown interest in her. But did her happiness not matter at all?

She looked at her father, imploring him to say something to suggest that he supported her and what she wanted, but he wouldn't meet her eyes, instead staring out the carriage window with the side of his ample cheek turned toward her. Helen sat across from her, staring at her feet as she attempted to ignore the conflict around her.

Olivia sat back and crossed her arms over her chest. She pursed her lips, saying nothing, but let the icy glare she shot at her mother speak for her. Her mother's words did give rise to the concerns Olivia had long held but didn't dare to speak aloud. What *would* she do with her life? She had her column in the Register. Could she grow her work enough to sustain herself one day? Her parents may no longer support her if they knew what she did, but she would have rewarding work, and be doing an activity that actually meant something and would make a difference. The idea began to percolate in her mind, and her mother shot her a glance of alarm at the sly smile that began to cross her face.

* * *

ALASTAIR FINCHLEY, the Duke of Breckenridge, did not want to attend this ball, a sentiment which was quite out of character. Alastair typically enjoyed these types of events, to have the opportunity to converse with the great variety of lords and ladies in attendance, during the moments he did not have a beautiful woman in his arms as he whirled around the dance floor.

Since his father had died, however, things had been different. He noticed now the way the mothers looked greedily at him as if he held the key to their daughter's futures. He saw how the young women stared at him as if they would do anything he asked, if only he would make them his bride. He also could not shake the idea that some of the other men now looked at him as more of a threat, believing marriage may be more imminent for him now that he was a duke.

He gave a wry laugh. If only these women knew what they would be getting — a duchy near to financial ruin and a man ill prepared to be a duke or a husband. He knew the answer to at least some of his problems were staring him in the face — he could marry one of those ladies with a large dowry, and bring an end to his short-term financial troubles while also taking on the responsibility that awaited him of beginning a family of his own.

The idea, however, sent a shiver down his spine. He did not want the responsibility of a wife, to have to worry about her wants and needs. Perhaps he could find a woman who would not care about the attention, or lack thereof, he provided to her. But even so, how could he enjoy himself in the company of others, women in particular, if he knew he had a wife waiting for him at home?

He was aware that he was known in society as somewhat of a rake for his love of women and the gambling hells, but he wasn't a true rogue in the sense of the word. He played by the rules, for the most part. He loved the art of seduction, but he was careful in the women he chose. He gambled, but not into debt. He drank, but not to the point that he made a fool of himself.

He set his turbulent thoughts aside and determined that tonight he would not worry so much and simply enjoy himself. He fixed his cravat, settled the sandy curls on his

HE'S A DUKE, BUT I LOVE HIM

head in some semblance of order, and made for the door to attend the ball in honor of Lady Sybille Grant at the Argyll Rooms, as the Grant's London home was not large enough to host such an event. His thoughts, unbidden, turned once again to Lady Olivia Jackson and a smile tugged at the corners of his previously down-turned mouth. She defied the conventions of society, which interested him, though not enough for him to consider anything more serious with her. She deserved better than him, more than a man who would leave her at home while he did as he pleased. He was not ready to give up the one aspect of his life that brought him pleasure, and he refused to be the man to break such a spirit as hers.

The smile remained on his face as he entered the magnificent front doors, lit by gilded lamps and bordered by Corinthian pillars, and passed his cloak to the butler. Alastair was soon greeted by Lord and Lady Grant. Lady Sybille was all smiles toward him, her youth and innocence and her mother's exuberance somewhat overwhelming.

He thanked them for having him before continuing through the crush of people into the ballroom, the din of chatter and the swell of the orchestra sweeping over him. He quickly found Lord Merryweather conversing among other gentlemen, and was welcomed into the circle with pats on the back and condolences, as this was the first true society event he had attended following his father's death.

He excused himself to find a drink, which he heartily needed, though his spirits began to be somewhat buoyed by the camaraderie and exuberance of those around him. He was returning to the group of gentleman when his path was blocked by voluminous skirts and the smiling faces of women of the *ton*.

"Ladies," he said with a slight bow toward them.

"We are ever so sorry to hear of the passing of your

father, Your Grace," said Lady Hester Montgomery, as she looked up at him from underneath forced fluttering eyelashes.

"Thank you, Lady Hester," he replied. "I appreciate it."

"It must be so difficult to be on your own during these troubling times," she said, placing a hand on his arm and practically leaning on him as her friend looked on with a similar smile plastered on her face. "Please call on me anytime should you need someone to talk to."

He nodded, and felt compelled to ask the woman if he might have a dance later that evening. She thrust a creamy white arm holding her dance card to him immediately. She was good-looking, dark-haired with brown eyes that flashed up at him eagerly. If she didn't throw off such an air of desperation, he might find himself more attracted to her.

She smiled up at him.

"I can hardly wait for our dance, Your Grace."

"Until then, Lady Hester," he said, and with a nod continued on his way.

* * *

THEY WERE LATE, as always. Olivia's mother felt if they arrived after most of the crowd, somehow it put them above everyone else awaiting them. Olivia thought it was ridiculous, but of course, her mother brushed aside her scoffing and her affable father found it easier to just follow along with what her mother wanted.

The ballroom looked beautiful, its bas-reliefs looking down on them from high upon the walls, the glass chandeliers shining overhead. Olivia thought she saw in Lady Grant the same hope and excitement that had been in her own mother's eyes five long years ago. Is that what they lived for?

She thought to herself, for their daughters to come out and find a husband? How depressing.

As she skirted the ballroom, Rosalind practically flew up toward her.

"Olivia! I have been waiting and waiting for you to tell me all about your adventure to the gambling house!"

"Shh," Olivia said with a quick look around to make sure no one had heard Rosalind's words. She led her over to a quieter corner of the room, away from interested ears.

Finally satisfied they would not be overheard, Olivia turned to her friend. "Oh Rosalind, it was wonderful," she said, her eyes shining.

"Was it truly?"

"Yes, absolutely," she responded, her excitement spilling over. "I played, and played well. Not just for fun, but it meant something. I didn't win on luck either, but I *earned* it."

"You always have been the intelligent one," said Rosalind with a sigh. "I am so envious. Not that I would ever take the risk that you did, but what fun. Did you see anyone you knew?"

"I did, actually," said Olivia slowly. "Lord Kenley — the Duke of Breckenridge."

"Oh, how interesting," Rosalind said with a knowing smile at her friend.

"It was nothing like that," Olivia denied. "He did recognize me. We were partnered, however, so I won him a good deal of money and for that I believe he will keep my secret."

"Mmm-hmmm," said Rosalind. "Is that the only reason? I heard how friendly you were at Isabella's house party last year. *And* you were at the Carrington dinner party last night — did you see him there as well?"

Olivia waved her words away with her hand and decided it was best to change the subject.

"There were other men present I recognized, of course,"

she said. "Fortunately I was able to stay far enough away from them, and besides that, most were too much in their cups to pay much notice of me. There was a moment I admit I believe I played a little too well as it seemed some of the men were not pleased with my winnings, but I managed to find the correct balance of success for the rest of the night."

"Very good, Olivia, very good," Rosalind said before her eyes turned to the dance floor. "Ah, look, there he is."

"There who is?"

"Why none other than your Duke — with Lady Hester."

CHAPTER 8

Olivia felt anger begin to simmer in her belly. Of everyone in this room, why did he have to dance with Hester Montgomery, the woman she could bear less than any other? Olivia saw the smug smile on the woman's face and her fingernails began to dig into the palms of her clenched hands.

Not — she told herself — that she was interested in the man himself. Clearly he was quite enamored with Lady Hester, as he smiled so charmingly at something she said, their faces just inches apart. Olivia noted the way Hester dropped her face to look coyly up at the Duke, and frustration tingled through her limbs.

"They do look well together," Rosalind said as she stood next to Olivia, who made a strangled noise from the back of her throat.

"I suppose they do," she said, as she unconsciously edged closer to the dance floor, though what she planned to do she didn't know. As she stood with her gaze on them, suddenly the Duke's eyes locked with hers over Hester's shoulder. He grinned, wide enough that she could see his dimple from where she stood, and he gave her a slow, steady wink. She gasped, and though her cheeks turned red, she was too stubborn to be the first to break eye contact.

"Olivia," Rosalind probed beside her, and Olivia finally turned to her.

"Yes?"

"Is something the matter?"

"No — nothing," she said, "Why do you ask?"

"You seem slightly upset," Rosalind said, her brow crinkling as the music of the set came to a close.

"Not at all," she answered, and as she turned to walk away from the dance floor, a strong hand suddenly warmed her arm through her long white glove.

"Lady Olivia?" his voice was rich and strong, and she cursed herself for the way it caused a tremor to flood through her, from her fingers and toes to the center of her belly.

She stilled her face into a small smile and looked up at him. "Your Grace, how lovely to see you."

"And you," he said, his green eyes hardening. "Do you have the next dance available?"

"You're lucky, Your Grace. For once — I do," she replied, and lifted her arm, her eyes widening as he filled his name in on the next two dance slots.

As they took to the floor for a waltz, she felt the lovely smile of Rosalind at her back, who melted back into the crowd to find her own betrothed, the cat-like smile that crossed her mother's face, and the burning glare of Lady Hester. Olivia looked at the woman from over the Duke's shoulder, and the leer Hester trained on her was one that promised retribution to come. Olivia raised her eyebrows and sent back a slight grin, before turning her attention to the man holding her in his arms.

"You look lovely tonight, Lady Olivia," he said, his

charming smile showcasing his straight white teeth. She looked up at him, wondering how she had missed the slightly crooked bottom teeth that offered character to the otherwise-perfect face.

"Thank you, Your Grace," she said. "You are looking well tonight yourself. Have your mother and sister accompanied you?'

"No," he replied. "It has not quite been a year since my father passed, so my mother is still in mourning. My sister remained home with her as she is awaiting my mother or a proper chaperone."

"Of course," Olivia responded, upset with herself for forgetting his recent loss as she had become caught up in the hardness of the muscle beneath her fingertips and his masculine scent of sandalwood and brandy that filled her.

"How respectable you look this evening, Lady Olivia," he said to her with a wicked grin.

"Did you expect otherwise?"

"One never seems to know what to expect when it comes to you."

"Is that such a terrible thing?"

"Not at all," he said with a smile. "In fact, I rather enjoy it. As I do your quick wit and intelligence. I am actually very taken by the workings of your mind."

"Those, Your Grace," she said, "are words to remember."

"You surprise me, Lady Olivia," he said. "I was under the impression that most women preferred words of compliment on their beauty and composure."

"You may find, Your Grace," she replied, "that I am not most women."

"No, Lady Olivia," he murmured, "you certainly are not."

* * *

When the dance ended, Alastair was grateful he'd had the foresight to sign his name on two slots of her dance card. He had forgotten how fun it was to flirt with Lady Olivia. It seemed, however, that something had shifted between them. It had been an innocent flirtation when they met at the house party. Now, following their most recent encounters, something simmered beneath the surface. It was a slow fire beginning to burn deeper, a desire for her that he was having trouble ignoring. He wasn't a stranger to such a feeling, but certainly not with a young woman of the *ton*.

It was the expression in her crystal-blue eyes, the way her pink lips responded to his teasing. Perhaps, he thought, one kiss of those lips and he would have her out of his system. Or would it possibly be too difficult to stop there? He wasn't sure, but he knew he could no longer stand here holding her so closely within the crush of people on the dance floor.

"Have you ever had the pleasure of touring the other areas of the Argyll Rooms?" he asked her as the orchestra readied for the next dance.

"I have not," she responded.

"Come, then, I must show you."

He saw her eyes narrow as if considering what he was about, but she seemed agreeable to the idea as her curiosity got the better of her and she placed her gloved fingers on his arm.

The building was fascinating, as Alastair saw it now through Lady Olivia's fresh eyes. She seemed to particularly enjoy the Blue Room, with the eagle soaring high above, atop the chandelier. He led her up the stairs, and they peeked in at the private boxes that surrounded the ballroom.

"There are 24 in total, I believe," he said. "They are primarily used when concerts and the like are hosted here."

Roman ox statues stood guard in front of each box. Those on the ground floor were ornamented with elegant antique bas-reliefs in bronze, and all were cloaked in scarlet draperies.

"Would you like to see the upper boxes?" he asked.

"Are they any different?" she responded, showing slight hesitation.

"They are," he said. "The upper tier is all the color of blue crystal."

Like her eyes, he thought, then shook his head at the foolish notion that had crossed his mind.

He led her up the stairs, and she gasped as she pushed back the scarlet draperies to see the box, the blue somewhat ethereal with the light of the beautiful circular bronze chandelier, its cut-glass pendants hanging down over them.

She walked further into the small space and he followed her, taking her hand and trailing behind her as he watched the expressions flit across her face.

* * *

Perhaps she should not be alone with him any longer. This was all rather untoward, and she knew she should have a chaperone. They should have remained in the ballroom. And yet … this was much more exciting.

"Lady Olivia…" he said, and pulled her around to face him. She turned with a smile, until she caught the serious look that crossed his normally upturned features. His hands moved from hers to her face, as he tipped her head back to look up at him. His thumbs grazed her cheeks, burning where they touched her. "Why do you captivate me so?"

"You do not find me off putting?"

He laughed. "You're interesting."

"I suppose that is meant as a compliment," she responded.

"Are you always so candid?" he asked.

"Of course," she said cheekily, "why do you think I'm still unmarried?"

Instead of answering, he leaned closer to her, so that she could feel the puff of his breath upon her cheek. He hesitated for a moment, as if allowing her time to pull away, but Olivia was never one to back down. Instead, she leaned in, meeting him part way as their lips met hungrily.

His mouth came down hard over hers, and her breath left her at the sudden intensity. His lips began moving, drinking her in, and Olivia felt the shock of it flood through her. He pressed her back against the wall, and when his tongue teased the seam of her lips, she willingly opened her mouth up to him. She matched his velvety smooth strokes, and soon a soft moan involuntarily left her lips. He broke the kiss for a moment, and she saw his head turning back and forth as if to ensure the draperies were closed around them, leaving them within their own private room.

He resumed the love play on her mouth and her hands reached up to twine in his hair. He lifted a hand to cup the bottom of her breast through her satin dress, his thumb flicking over her nipple that had her pressing into him with reckless abandon.

"Your Grace," she breathed out.

"Alastair," he responded, working a breast free, up out of the fabric that covered it. He cupped it, gently rubbing a finger over it as he kissed her once more. As she pressed into him instinctively, however, he pulled back rather suddenly.

"Olivia, we must stop," he said, his breathing ragged.

"Why?" she asked, feeling the heat rising through her body to her cheeks, which must be quite reddened by now.

"Because — because you are a lady, an innocent, and I am — well I am not looking for a wife, and that is certainly where something like this would lead with a woman like you."

"A woman like me?" she raised an eyebrow.

"Yes. One does not toy with the daughter of an earl."

"You are not toying with me, Your Grace. I am an equal part of this equation."

"So you are," he said, "even so —"

She kept him from speaking as she reached up and laced her fingers behind his head, pulling his lips back down to hers. He groaned and lost himself in her kisses until a nose behind him startled him and he jumped back. The curtain keeping them within their inner sanctuary had suddenly been thrown open — they were no longer alone.

CHAPTER 9

"Olivia!"

Olivia pushed back from the Duke, as he hurriedly did all he could to cover her bared breast.

"M-Mother?"

For once in her life, Olivia struggled for words as she looked into her mother's face. This is not so terrible, she thought. Her mother would keep this to herself, for she would never want the scandal to —

The drapery was pushed back further and Lady Hester, accompanied by two of her friends, entered the room that felt tinier by the moment.

"Why Lady Olivia," she purred out. "This is quite the scandal, is it not?"

It seemed a slight crowd had gathered outside the private box, and Olivia stood still in shock. "This is — that is…"

"Lady Olivia and I were dancing and she needed some time away from the crowd," the Duke cut in, in an attempt to explain.

"So instead," said Lady Sutcliffe, her shrewd eyes taking

them both in, "you decided to take my daughter into a private box and ruin her?"

"Ruin? Oh, Mother, don't say such a thing!"

"What do you suppose this means for you?" asked Lady Sutcliffe, turning sharply toward her. "You are caught with your bosom half hanging out of your gown in a closeted room, your hair askew and a man's hands on you. No matter what dowry we provide you, you will never find a husband after this — besides the Duke, of course."

She gave him a smug smile.

"Mother!" Olivia hissed, "Don't do this. We will discuss it later — in private."

"Yes," she said, her eyebrows raised, "we will. My husband will be expecting you tomorrow, Your Grace. Now come Olivia, I believe it's time we leave."

Olivia, for once, did as she was told, following her mother out the door without a backward look at the Duke, the room silent but for the sputters of laughter from Lady Hester and her friends.

"Do shut up, Hester," she said, unable to keep her mouth closed in parting as she turned the corner and left the room, holding her head high.

The carriage ride home was absolutely silent, as Olivia sat looking out the window, not saying a word to her family. She reviewed the events of the evening over and over in her mind. She wasn't sure what had come over her. When the Duke had kissed her, she had lost all thought and acted strictly on instinct and emotion. When she followed him up the stairs to the private box, she was well aware of what she was doing, of what could happen on their own. She remembered having the thought streak through her mind that this moment of adventure, of excitement, was worth whatever consequences would come her way.

Besides, she didn't want a husband anyway, so what did it

matter if she was ruined? She could withstand the gossip and titters of Lady Hester and the like. She settled back against the squabs and closed her eyes, preparing herself for the coming battle.

*　*　*

"I WILL NOT MARRY HIM."

She stood in the drawing room, facing her parents, her mother sitting on the soft rose sofa with her hands folded in her lap, her father standing behind her, a united front. Helen sat in the corner of the sofa beside her mother, while Olivia faced them all, her hands on her hips and her feet planted firmly onto the lush carpet.

She had spent the night tossing and turning as she contemplated her current predicament. At one point she had risen and paced her room, staring out the window as if she would find her answers in the stars hanging above London.

She eventually determined that she would refuse to be pushed into a corner, trapped into marriage with a very-handsome, yet very-rakish duke. The man was well known for his womanizing ways, and Olivia would not be the idiot wife who sat at home turning a blind eye to her husband's dalliances. She would rather be a spinster for the rest of her life.

She must now make her parents understand her point of view. She wasn't quite at the point to support herself without them, so she had to ensure she could stay under their roof for the time being.

"Olivia, be reasonable," her mother harped back at her. "By now all of Society will be well aware of your dalliance with the Duke. You will never respectably marry now — likely not ever."

"That's fine," Olivia replied, her nose in the air. "I do not need to marry."

Her mother snorted. "Do not be obstinate. Of course you want to marry — every woman does."

"Not every woman, Mother," Olivia responded, bending to look her mother directly in the eye. "I certainly do not."

"Why not?" her mother asked with a laugh. "What else do you propose to do with your life?"

"I will work," she said with a shrug.

"Work?" her mother actually let out a laugh this time. "Where do you suppose you will work?"

"That is none of your concern," responded Olivia, turning her head to look out the window to collect her thoughts.

Her mother attempted a different tactic.

"This is the best opportunity you will ever be offered. The Duke of Breckenridge! Do you know how many women would be willing to trade places with you?"

"First of all," began Olivia, as she paced back and forth down the carpet, the eyes of her family members following her as if she were an actress commanding the stage. "The Duke has not offered for me yet, so this may all be for naught. Secondly, you must know the Duke's propensity for women. You would really have me married to a man who would likely spend much of his time with all other sorts of women?"

As she looked at her parents expectantly, her mother stared straight back at her, and unblinkingly shrugged while her father, at least, was unable to meet her eye.

"Father?" she said, looking at him for support.

"Olivia," he began hesitatingly. "You know that I have supported you these past years as you have sought out a love match."

Her mother sniffed loudly, as if to remind them all that *she* certainly had not been a proponent of this.

"Yes," she replied. "And I do appreciate so much all you have done for me. Most fathers would not have been as understanding."

He inclined his head toward her. "That being said, it is far past time that you do marry. As for working, I am proud of your intelligence, Olivia, especially as a woman, however that cannot provide support for you for the rest of your life. Certainly not in the style to which you are accustomed."

Her face fell at her father's words. If anyone had ever believed in her, it was he.

"But —"

He didn't let her finish. "We must also consider Helen."

"Helen?"

"Yes. You know that while it is expected that you marry first, Helen has still had the opportunity to find a suitable match regardless of your status. Now, however, should you be ruined and unmarried ... Helen will not have much chance at all for a respectable marriage."

Olivia stopped the flow of words that were close to spilling out of her mouth and turned to her sister. They had never been particularly close, as they were so very different and rather far apart in age, but Olivia did feel a great deal of affection toward her, and had always felt her quiet and timid sister was something of her responsibility. Should she keep her from marriage…?

"Helen," she prodded, "what are your thoughts on this situation?"

Helen looked up at her with a sheen of unshed tears covering her eyes.

"Please Olivia," she whispered, "do not ruin us."

Olivia's breath caught in her throat at the impassioned plea. Don't ruin *us*, her sister had said. In all of this, she had never stopped to consider that element.

"Very well," she said, the words practically forced out of her lips. "I shall marry him."

* * *

Alastair paced around his study, his thoughts swirling round his head. He was angry at himself, hardly believing he had allowed his body's desires to overtake all rational thought at the ball. This was why he had kept himself away from Lady Olivia Jackson. She was the one woman among the young, unmarried ladies of the *ton* who intrigued him. He had thought one chaste kiss would be enough to get her out of his thoughts, but it had the opposite effect. Not only had the kiss turned to passion, but now that he had tasted her, he wanted more.

More is certainly what he could get if he followed the direction of the Countess, he thought with a wry grin. Alastair hated being told what to do. His father had attempted to order him around throughout his entire life, and Alastair despised being manipulated. Not only that, he had no wish at all to be married.

But as ready — or not — as he was, did he still have a choice? He may be known for his propensity for women, but that did not mean that he was ever out to ruin young ladies. But ruin he did. Lady Olivia would never find a suitable match after this. Too many had been witness to their tryst.

Alastair frowned as he realized it was more than likely that her mother had known exactly what she would find when she pushed aside the curtain with the crowd of people behind her. Lady Sutcliffe had *wanted* to see her daughter ruined. The thought made Alastair sick. Did he really want to be part of such a family?

A knock on the door startled him out of his reverie, and he marched over to open it, finding his mother on the other side, still dressed in black as part of her mourning ritual for his father.

"Mother," he nodded his head at her.

She gave him a kiss on the cheek as she entered the room, and sat in one of his wingback chairs to look up at him. She looked very out of place in this masculine room that had been his father's domain to rule for so many years. His mother was still a beautiful woman, despite the stark black costume and the gray that tinged her hair. She had managed to retain much of her joy for life, despite his father trying his best to stamp it out of her for years.

It was where, he supposed, he had found his own levity.

"How was the ball last evening?" she questioned him, a soft smile on her face.

"You heard?" he asked with a sigh, wandering over to the sideboard and pouring himself a glass of brandy, despite the fact it was well before noon. "Word travels quickly."

"It does," she said with a nod, "particularly when the Countess of Sutcliffe is intent on ensuring it travels."

He rolled his eyes and took a sip, letting the brandy burn down his throat.

"The woman was entirely too pleased about her daughter's ruination," he said to his mother.

"Yes, I could see Lady Sutcliffe not protesting her daughter's entanglement with a duke," his mother said, leaning back against the arm of the chair. "What are you going to do?"

"I don't know, Mother," he said, rubbing his aching temple with the index and middle fingers of his right hand. "I have no desire to find myself wed anytime soon."

"Tell me, Alastair, do you believe the girl had any intent of trapping you into marriage?"

"No," he responded immediately. "She had no way of

knowing what would transpire and she was truly angry with her mother."

"It is no longer my place to tell you what to do," she said slowly. "However, I believe, in your heart, you know what the right decision is."

"Yes," he said, a sickening feeling deepening in the pit of his stomach. "I believe I do."

CHAPTER 10

The knock on the door came but an hour after Olivia had made her decision.

The family was still gathered in the drawing room, the air around them filled with tension. While her mother and Helen embroidered and her father sat reading the morning papers, Olivia had moved to lie on the window seat with a book in her lap, her gaze out the window on the street below, and her mind somewhere else completely.

Upon the Duke's arrival, her father left the drawing room to speak with him in his study. Olivia nervously bit her fingernails as she waited for them both. How ridiculous that two men should be deciding her future as she sat here like an idiot. There was nothing, however, she could currently do about the matter, and so she waited, albeit impatiently.

As she swung her leg back and forth over the window seat, she determined how best to approach this marriage — how she could still have her freedom while ensuring her sister's future remained secure. She came to a resolute decision, feeling she had all the practicalities of the situation arranged in her mind. Then the Duke was shown in.

It seemed as if all the air had been sucked out of the room when he entered, for she couldn't quite seem to catch her breath as he stood framed in the doorway, the light from the tall window shining off the golden tones of his sandy curls. Olivia felt heat climbing through her cheeks as she sat rooted to her seat, staring at the man who had brought such passionate feelings forth from her only the previous night. She took in his strong, hard body, the chest she had run her hands over, the silken locks of his hair she had intertwined her fingers through, and the lips that had shown her what desire really meant.

His slight nod to her finally broke the spell that had overcome her, and her rampant desire was replaced by guilt and regret over their actions from the night before, and her mother's discovery that had forced them into this situation.

A hiss from Lady Sutcliffe finally brought Olivia to her feet, and she curtsied ridiculously as the Duke stepped into the room, followed closely by her father.

"Your Grace," her mother purred, clasping her hands together in front of her, "how lovely to see you."

As if he had called upon them out of societal politeness.

"My lady," he said, inclining his head toward her, although none could miss the frost that cloaked his eyes as he regarded her.

"Well," the Earl began, in an attempt to cut through the stiffness that had engulfed them all. "It is settled. His Grace will marry Olivia as soon as a special license can be procured. We shall have the ceremony in the parlor, I believe, as it shall be a small, private affair."

He beamed and gave a nod of his head to them all. Olivia let out a small snort at her parents' reaction, as if this had been a proper courtship and betrothal of two parties, while nothing could be further from the truth. The Duke, a pained expression on his usually jovial face, looked far from a man delighted to be entering matrimonial bliss. And she, well, she would have nothing to do with this if it weren't for her younger sister.

"May I have a moment alone with the Duke?" Her voice rang out through the room, which became silent but for the ticking of the long-case clock from the landing and the footsteps of servants in the corridor as they all turned toward her.

"I suppose it does not make much difference any longer," her mother said in a clipped tone. "Come, Helen."

Her sister meekly followed her mother out the door, as did her father, though he stopped to give the Duke a pointed glare. The Duke inclined his head, silently acknowledging the warning her father gave.

When the door clicked behind them, Olivia was once again very aware of the presence of the tall, broad man she had so eagerly fallen into the arms of the night before.

As fast as her heart beat, she refused to turn in fear from this man who would soon become her husband, and she looked up at him, meeting the jeweled tone of his eyes.

"I will have you know, Your Grace, that none of this was my intention," she said, a determined set to her chin. "In fact, I would not have agreed to marriage were it not for my sister."

"Your sister?" he inclined an eyebrow.

"Yes," she responded. "I care not for my own ruination, but I do not want to see Helen affected by ... the scandal. She is out now herself and she would very much like a husband of her own. I do not want to bring such disgrace to our family so as to affect her prospects."

He cleared his throat.

"I must apologize, Lady Olivia," he said, his voice polite and stilted, the voice of a stranger and not the warm baritone to which she was so accustomed. "I should have put more thought into my actions before taking you into that blasted box."

"Yes, well…" she said, a slight smile touching her lips, "one cannot say I was not in agreement."

The silence stretched between them.

"Was that all you wished to say to me?" he questioned.

"Yes. No. I — I know this is not what you want," she began, now unable to meet his eyes. "If you wish a marriage in name only, I shall understand, however … however I need to know this from the beginning."

"Why?" His one-word question had her eyes flinging up to meet his.

"Why?" she repeated dully. "So I know … how to regard you."

He gave a grunt of derision. "And how do you currently regard me, Lady Olivia?"

The heat filled her cheeks once more as she took a few steps away from the safety of her window view toward him. "I regard you as a man who enjoys the company of women. Many women. Who has made well known his disregard for marriage and who would prefer to remain a bachelor. Who now finds himself betrothed to a woman because he was caught acting upon his desires, and who now regrets ever leaving the ballroom at the Argyll Rooms."

* * *

As Alastair listened to Olivia's words, he realized how very true they were. He knew the gossip, the words that had likely been whispered into her ears about him. And yet he had never truly cared about it. Never, that is, until this moment when the words came forth from her lips to his ears.

They rattled something within him, something that made

him want to refute what she was saying, and yet, he could not. For he did enjoy women, he did not want to marry, and he would prefer to remain a bachelor. Somehow despite the truth in what she said, however, he did not regret those moments in the box at the Argyll Rooms. When he had kissed her, the feeling that charged through him was unlike any he had ever felt before. He didn't want to marry her, no — but yet he couldn't deny he still ached for her.

"I can see I'm not incorrect in my assumptions," she continued, her tones now crisp and businesslike, not unlike those of her mother's from just minutes earlier. "Very well, then. I shall make an agreement with you, one that will benefit us both. We shall marry, in name only, to save both our reputations. However, you may choose to do as you wish — visit your clubs, gamble your money, t-take your women. In turn, I may choose to do as I please. You will not question me, or provide me with orders. I will not bring shame to your name, but nor will I be at your every command. Agreed?"

She raised her eyebrows expectantly and stared serenely upon him, as he stood in shocked silence looking at her. To be married in name only ... he couldn't deny that the one aspect of this wedding he had been looking forward to was bedding his soon-to-be wife. And yet the offer she provided him was quite tempting. He could continue living as he wished, and in turn he had to do nothing but leave her be? But of course — he didn't wish to have responsibility for another, and by each of them taking their freedoms they could have what they both wanted.

He smiled his first true smile since Lady Sutcliffe had strode in upon them yesterday.

"Agreed."

CHAPTER 11

The wedding was, as the Earl had described, a small and simple affair. Olivia dressed in her most elaborate gown, a deep blue silk that brought out the crystal of her eyes. Her maid, Molly, came to Olivia with a fabulous, intricate design for her hair in mind, but Olivia shook her head and requested a simple chignon instead. Molly protested, but Olivia's determination won out, and she was pleased with the effect of the simple style above the high-waisted dress, with its puffed sleeves and plaits.

She descended the stairs to the parlor, where her father met her at the door. She peeked her head inside, seeing the large room had been slightly reconfigured to accommodate the small number of people who congregated. There were her mother and sister, of course, and the Duke's mother, still dressed in black, along with a young woman who she took to be his sister in half-mourning clothes. There were a few people she did not recognize, who must be related to the Duke or perhaps his friends, and two of her own cousins, including the one who would inherit this estate one day. She felt a rush of relief to see Rosalind and her fiancé, as well as

Isabella and her husband. She had written them in haste yesterday, hopeful they would be in attendance to provide some comfort on this day.

"Are you prepared for this, daughter?" her father asked somewhat gently as he smiled at her.

"As prepared as I shall be," she replied, her face set resolutely.

"Olivia..." he said, hesitatingly. "I know this is not what you want. But please, child, do try to be happy."

She didn't look him in the eye, but responded, "Let us begin."

He nodded and walked her to the vicar standing before the guests, where the Duke of Breckenridge awaited her.

He inclined his head toward her, and gave her a characteristic wink to somewhat ease the tension that filled the room, as all in attendance were well aware of the circumstances.

The vicar cleared his throat and began, seeming somewhat pleased when no one objected to this wedding. Apparently he had his doubts as well. Olivia managed to keep her emotions in check, until the time came for their vows.

The vicar turned to the Duke. "Wilt thou have this woman to thy wedded wife, to live together after God's ordinance in the holy estate of Matrimony? Wilt thou love her, comfort her, honor, and keep her in sickness and in health; and, forsaking all others, keep thee only unto her, so long as ye both shall live?"

The Duke's face remained impassive, until the line of "forsaking all others," when a muscle in his cheek twitched and his eyes turned from hers.

"I will," he said quietly.

"And wilt thou have this man to thy wedded husband, to live together after God's ordinance in the holy estate of Matrimony? Wilt thou obey him, and serve him, love, honor, and keep him in sickness and in health; and, forsaking all others, keep thee only unto him, so long as ye both shall live?"

Olivia winced at the words to "obey him, and serve him," to which the Duke's lips turned upwards in a slight smile which only she could see. She swallowed a lump in her throat as she responded, "I will."

The remainder of the ceremony drew forward in somewhat of a blur, until the final words were read and Olivia found herself suddenly turned to face the guests of her wedding. And with that, she realized, she was a duchess, married — in name, at least, to this man beside her, a man she had wanted feverishly, and yet did not want to find herself bound to. Her mother had always said her yearn for adventure would be her undoing. As it turned out, she was right.

"Smile," came the rich voice in her ear, the one that sent shivers down her spine.

She did, but the smile did not quite reach her eyes. She had posed this agreement to him, not accounting for the depths of her desire for him. She knew, however, she must not give in. For to do so, to acknowledge any sort of feeling toward him, be it lust or any other emotion, would be her undoing. For if she felt anything for this man, the only result would be her own broken heart. No. She must keep herself far, far away. After this blasted wedding breakfast was over.

* * *

"Come, come!" said the Earl, rising and clapping his hands once the vows were complete. "We must now celebrate this wonderful union that has taken place today. We invite you all to the dining room for a breakfast together."

Olivia's parents bestowed handshakes and smiles on each

of the wedding guests, while Alastair's mother looked at him with raised eyebrows as if to ask if this was what was expected — to follow along as if nothing was amiss. He smiled and shrugged his shoulders at her, silently responding with a yes.

It had certainly been an interesting ceremony, as he reflected on the vows they spoke to one another. As much as Olivia questioned his loyalty to her, he had always been of the mind that when he did marry — which he had hoped would be far into the future, but no mind of that now — he *would* be faithful to his wife. He had been prepared for that today, until Olivia came to him with her surprising suggestion. Now he was unsure how to go forward. If she didn't want him at all, then what was he to do? He couldn't very well live as a monk.

The dining room was as horrid as the remainder of the house. The wallpaper that could be seen from beneath the paintings and portraits hung about him was a floral pattern in a pale rose and crimson red, which clashed horribly with the deep purple upholstery of the chairs around the table. Alastair was not typically one to notice the color of one's decor, but even he could not help but wrinkle his nose at it.

"I say," said his sister in his ear, as she walked by him to her own chair. "This house is simply dreadful!"

He shushed her even as he smiled, but his grin faded as he turned to see Olivia, sitting next to him, had heard the exchange and was staring at them both with her eyebrows raised. Anne looked horrified as she realized what Olivia had heard.

"Olivia — that is, Your Grace — I am every so sorry, I —"

Olivia waved her hand as she surprised them both by chuckling. "If there is one thing I shall not miss," she said in a low, conspiratorial tone, "it is this awful house."

Anne's worried face disappeared in relief, and Alastair

had to be grateful to his new wife for putting his sister at ease.

"Oh ,and Anne," she added as the girl continued on her way. "Please, never call me 'Your Grace.' Olivia will do ever so nicely."

"Of course, Olivia," Anne said with a wide smile, and Alastair knew that Olivia had forever endeared herself to the girl.

The breakfast was as fine as could be expected. He did not speak often to Olivia, unsure of what exactly he would say to her. He watched as she twirled the simple band round her finger over and over, the piece of metal unfamiliar, and now a reminder that they were bound to one another for the rest of their lives. His throat somewhat constricted at the thought, and he pushed it aside as he concentrated on answering a question the Earl posed to him regarding his thoughts on the latest horse race.

"Unfortunately, I do not gamble on horses," he responded. He preferred the card table, where he had some semblance of control, unlike the track where it was all based on the luck of choosing the right horse, and where his father had lost so much of their fortune.

"Fair enough," said the Earl with a wave of his fork. "You are a smart lad."

Alastair nodded, and once the cake was served, he drew out his pocket watch to determine if the hour was reasonable enough for them to make their excuses and be going. He pushed back his chair to stand and announce his departure when Lady Sutcliffe stood and called all of their attention.

He thought he heard Olivia groan beside him, but perhaps he was imagining it, so faint was the sound.

"Th-thank you all for coming," she said with a slight hiccup, and Alastair frowned. It seemed the lady had drunk one too many glasses of wine with her breakfast. He hoped the Earl would intercede and spare them all the embarrassment that was to come, but unfortunately, it was not to be so.

"While it was a lovely ceremony," she said, as Alastair noted a slight weave to her countenance, "I would so have loved my eldest daughter to have married a duke at St. George's instead of the parlor. Well, Olivia was never one to do as she ought, that is for certain. I suppose I should just be thankful that she ruined herself with a man of such a lovely title!"

"Mother!" said Olivia sharply, and her father did take the opportunity to sit his wife down.

"I believe what my wife means to say," he said, his cheeks red, "is that we appreciate you all being present for our daughter's marriage to the Duke of Breckenridge. We are pleased to join our families together."

Olivia stoically sat beside him, not saying a word, as if this display was somehow not quite unexpected. His own mother looked fairly horrified, while Anne looked positively thrilled. Olivia's own sister, Helen, he believed her name was, simply sat staring at her plate as she had throughout most of the meal. How could two women be so closely related and yet so utterly different?

No matter. He realized then exactly why Olivia had felt it so important to continue with the marriage. Her sister likely did not entertain many suitors as it was. A scandal would positively ruin her. It was, perhaps, somewhat noble what Olivia had done, and he felt guilty for his role in forcing her into this marriage.

There was certainly nothing he could do about it now, however. He reflected on her preposterous suggestion. He supposed it could be done, he thought, though he had been looking forward to bedding his wife tonight. Perhaps he would pay her a visit and see how she responded. A grin flew over his lips. He could seduce her. He had done it before, and she seemed willing and eager enough.

His mind quickly overcame his body's desire. *No.* He would not take advantage of the situation they found themselves in. He would make love to her when — and not if, for he knew she felt something for him — she desired him in turn, however long that would be.

And if she truly did not want him? Well, then, he would have to consider his options.

CHAPTER 12

Olivia felt the post-nuptial celebration, despite the most unconventional dialogue and her mother's drunken speech, had actually gone much better than she could have hoped. The Duke was his usual charming self, and his mother and sister were actually quite lovely. Her own mother, for the most part, had pasted on a charming facade for the Duke's family, and Olivia was content spending time with both Rosalind and Isabella.

Yes, it all went very well, except for the fact that she and the Duke had barely spoken.

It had felt quite strange to leave her family's London home with the Finchley family — *her* family now, she realized. She had said goodbye to her mother with little emotion, and had given Helen a sweet smile, whispering in her ear for her to keep her chin up and not let their mother have her way all the time. The only tear that escaped her eye was when her father had enveloped her in a tight embrace. He'd always treated her as more than a daughter, with the respect near to what a son would garner. She would miss sitting with him in the library or his study as they each poured over their books.

She was about to leave when he called her back for a moment. "Olivia," he said, then brought her close and murmured in a voice that only she could hear, "Keep up the good work, my little P.J. Scott."

She gasped and stared at him in astonishment. How had he known? But he only winked at her and turned her to the door, where her husband awaited to accompany her to his — their — home in the Breckenridge coach, their crest etched on the side.

The Duke's sister, Anne, chattered the entire way back to their home, about how lovely the ceremony was and how romantic was their quick marriage. She could not wait to tell her friends all about it, and questioned the Duke as to how long would they remain in London so that she might perhaps find her own husband this year? She seemed so eager to re-enter society herself, her first season abruptly cut short by her father's death, and asked Olivia how many seasons she had been out for.

"Five," Olivia responded.

Anne gasped. "My goodness, that is quite a few!"

"Yes," Olivia said with a wry grin. "I have heard that before."

"Oh, my apologies," Anne said, her cheeks turning pink. "I never meant anything by it. Besides, I suppose it all worked out for you with my brother."

"Yes," Olivia said with a nod, "I suppose it did."

The Finchley's London manor was quite grand, and had been in the family for many years. As Olivia spent the majority of the remainder of the day exploring the home, she felt the eyes of the Duke's ancestors staring at her from their portraits on the wall. Dinner was a small affair following the extravagant breakfast from earlier in the day, and the Duke remained fairly silent as Olivia chattered with Anne, finding themselves well suited to one another.

Olivia felt for the girl, who was so eager to begin life as a young woman of the *ton*, and yet had continued to be delayed through no fault of her own. Olivia resolved to speak with Alastair to ensure that Anne could return to events in due time. She herself could now accompany her as a chaperone. How amusing, she thought, that she would now be eligible to act as chaperone. It had been six months since the death of the former Duke of Breckenridge, and while Olivia knew the pain was likely still there, it was a reasonable amount of time to reappear in society.

She retired early that evening, making her way alone upstairs and down the hallway to her new bedchamber.

Olivia wondered what it must be like for the Dowager Duchess to have her in the home, assuming what presumably had once been her chambers when her husband was alive. No matter, though, she was pleasant to her and seemed genuinely welcoming.

Her maid, Molly, who had left her parents' employ to come with her to her new home, had arranged most of Olivia's clothing and possessions within the chamber. Olivia felt that the sooner she had her own things in the space, the sooner she would feel more comfortably at home. Already, however, she far preferred the decor of this house to her parents'. The white walls set off the crimson beddings and curtains, while the mahogany armoire and dressing table were rich and inviting. Mercifully, there was no pink to be found anywhere in the room.

"You looked beautiful today, Lady Olivia — that is, Your Grace," her maid said as she took the pins out of Olivia's hair, letting it fall to her shoulders in cascading waves before beginning to pleat it.

HE'S A DUKE, BUT I LOVE HIM

"Oh Molly, Your Grace sounds so formal and you have known me for far too long. Olivia is fine," she said to the girl.

Molly nodded but seemed unsure, though she chatted on about the beauty of the new home as she helped Olivia undress and step into her nightgown and wrapper. "Your husband is very handsome," she said, then as a blush rose in her cheeks, added, "My apologies, my lady, that was far too forward of me."

"Not to worry Molly," she said with a twist of a smile. "You're not the only woman to feel that way."

With a confused look on her face, Molly opened her mouth to speak, but before any words came out, a knock sounded at the door adjoining her bedroom to her husband's. "Oh!" Molly said, her hand flying to her lips. "That must be him. If that will be all?"

"Yes," Olivia said, turning back on her seat toward the mirror as Molly opened the door and scurried down the hall before Olivia bid the Duke to enter.

He cleared his throat from behind her.

"Wife," he said, his eyebrows rising as she turned to face him.

"I have a name," she said, looking up at him, her eyes crystallizing. "Olivia."

"Very well, Olivia," he said, her name sounding nearly foreign the way he rolled it off his tongue. "And you must call me Alastair."

She nodded.

"You looked very beautiful today," he said, the enchanting grin back on his face, although Olivia could see it did not quite meet his eyes.

"There is no need to charm me, Alastair," she responded. "I meant what I said today. A civil arrangement will suit me fine."

And will keep my fickle heart from falling for you, only to be broken, she thought.

Suddenly she realized the reason why he may be here, in her chamber.

"Unless, that is, you feel it necessary tonight to...."

"No, no," he said, his hand sweeping out in front of him. "I do not expect anything from you, unless you should choose it."

She looked up at him, at the olive tones of his skin visible where he had already removed his cravat, showing the smooth lines of his chest, and the strength in his legs underneath the tight-fitting breeches that left little to her imagination, though her mind roamed there anyway. She remembered the way her hands had roamed over his strong jaw, and entwined in his stylish tawny hair, shorter on the sides, but curling on top. She felt a pull deep inside her that longed to say, yes, please, give me a wedding night. She yearned for his hands on her body, craved to feel his lips on hers again. Their hurried kisses in the Argyll Rooms had not been enough. She wanted more, wanted him.

But it could not be. For she knew herself. Whatever emotion she felt was typically strong and passionate, be it exuberance, sorrow, anger, or love. She did not have a great deal of control over her sentiments, and if she gave him her body she would be giving him part of herself, and she would desire more than just the physical connection. And with a man like him, that could only ever lead to heartbreak.

"I believe ... I feel that for now I would prefer our arrangement to remain according to the terms we set out this morning," she said, her eyes on the oriental rug that adorned the floor of her room.

"Very well," he said. "Goodnight, then ... Olivia."

"Goodnight, Alastair."

With that, he turned on his heel and returned to his

chamber, closing the door behind him and leaving Olivia feeling slightly bereft and completely alone. It was her own fault, however, and she resolved it was time to sleep and she would feel much better come morning.

She had never been one to take to bed early, however. How many nights had she spent hours in the library, studying or working on her articles, while the rest of the house slept around her? She loved this time of day, the time when she could do as she pleased without her mother looking over her shoulder or a servant ready to respond to her every need. She was actually, truly, well and completely alone and she should rejoice in it, not feel sorrowful, she told herself.

She picked up the candle on the side table by her bed, and first put her ear to the door adjoining her chamber to Alastair's. She could hear his footsteps within, telling her he was there, and she slowly opened the room's other door which led to the hall, shoving her long blonde braid behind her shoulder.

She looked one way and the other, but seeing no one, she began down the hall and tiptoed down the stairs as she tried to recall where the library was located. It didn't take long for her to find the room, and she eased open the door, pleased to find it dark and empty. She used her own candle to light others in the room and take a better look around.

It did not boast the bookshelves of her father's own library, but it did include a sizeable desk as well as comfortable dark-brown leather and walnut wingback chairs and a matching thick window seat that overlooked the street below. She wandered around the room, finally coming to sit on the edge of the seat. She curled her legs below her as she looked out on the Mayfair streets of London. She set no light beside her so that she would not be visible to any passersby, but instead took her fill of all that stood out below. The hour being late, there was little activity outside, but the gas street lamps provided pools of light, accented by the dim light falling from windows of homes whose occupants were similarly awake.

She saw movement underneath her, and she rose as she leaned forward to see who it might be as she took in a form emerging from the doorway below her. When he walked beneath the streetlamp, she swallowed hard as she realized it was Alastair, providing instructions to the groom as he entered his carriage.

She felt a pang in her chest. It was her wedding night, and her groom was off to heaven only knew where. A club, a gaming hall, a — a mistress? Her heart skipped a beat. Did it really matter? She had told him this is what she wanted, nothing but an arrangement. He had come to her bedchamber, providing her with the invitation for a wedding night, and she had refused. So why did this streak of jealousy tear through her?

Because she wanted him to want her, despite her refusal to him, which she knew made no sense whatsoever. It was bad luck on his part that he had been caught with a young, unwed woman of society. He had paid for it with marriage, but he would not change his life.

Olivia stood, cursing herself for the foolish emotions wreaking havoc on all rational thought. Her jealousy was not only for want of Alastair's desire, but also for the easy way which he passed through the night. He could travel throughout the city at any hour he pleased, without comment or repercussion. Were she to be found doing the same, however, it could mean scandal and ruin. Well, additional scandal and ruin, she thought, rolling her eyes.

She meandered back through the library and the corridor to her rooms. As she shut the door behind her, she steeled herself with new resolve to keep Alastair far, far away, and not let a sliver of him enter her soul.

* * *

As he entered the gaming hall, Alastair was soon greeted by lords of his acquaintance, as well as the card dealers and serving girls who knew him. He was not a regular visitor, but he did find himself in an establishment such as this from time to time when he was looking for a bit of fun.

He had entered the rooms of his wife this evening unsure of what to expect. Had she seemed to want him, he would have celebrated his wedding night in typical fashion. But the usual talkative Olivia Jackson — no, Olivia Finchley now — had not been the woman with whom he had flirted, danced, and kissed. Instead, she had been replaced by a much more cold and tight-lipped version of herself, at least when she was addressing him. After she had dismissed him, he had paced his room for a few minutes before feeling the need to escape it, and soon had ended up here.

Lord Merryweather approached him shortly, greeting him with a slap on the back. "Breckenridge! Congratulations on your wedding this morning, man. But whatever are you doing here, in a gaming hell, on your wedding night?"

Alastair gave his friend a rueful grin.

"I think marriage will take some time to grow on me," he said. "In the meantime, what's the harm in having a bit of fun?"

Merryweather shrugged his shoulders, though he did give Alastair a bit of a sideways glance.

They made their way to the faro table, though as they passed the men playing whist, Alastair thought of his beautiful blonde wife and her expertise in the game. Perhaps if nothing else she could provide him with a bit of education on how to become as proficient as she.

As the game began, his opponent soon had a serving girl sitting on his lap. Serving girl was a bit of a loose term, as the women in this club certainly served more than drinks. Another scantily clad woman brought Alastair his brandy, asking him with a sly smile if he would like anything else.

He smiled at her. She was certainly attractive with midnight-black hair and a dress leaving very little to the imagination. He opened his mouth to agree, but the words seemed to stall on his lips. The usual desire he might feel for such a woman did not seem to be present. Instead, he felt … guilty. He had a wife at home, an alluringly stunning woman who many a man would be grateful for, and here he was considering a whore in a club. When he thought of making love to a woman, the only image that came into his mind was a blonde with a wide smile, generous hips and crystal-blue eyes. He shook his head at the woman and she moved off with a backward glance.

Alastair gave a slight growl of frustration. *This* was why he did not want a wife. Sure, she may tell him this marriage was just an arrangement, but that did not change his unease at the entire situation. He was a cad, or would be should he continue to find his desires slaked elsewhere. And yet *she* certainly seemed to no longer have any interest in him.

He sighed and threw down a card. He didn't know what was to happen next, but one thing was for certain — the life he had known was over.

CHAPTER 13

Olivia sailed into the dining room the next morning, seeming to purposefully time her entrance so that Alastair was nearly finished with his breakfast, yet would now have to politely wait for her. His mother typically broke her fast in her rooms, and Anne had long since eaten. The footman pulled out Olivia's chair and she sat with the flourish of a queen, smiling broadly at her husband.

"Good morning, darling," she said as she picked up her teacup.

"Good morning, Olivia," he responded, looking warily up at her as if he knew something was afoot. "What has caused you to be in such high spirits this morning?"

"It must simply be newly wedded bliss," she said with a dainty sip. "And how was your evening last night?"

"Fine," he said without any elaboration. He did not want to speak to her of last night. It had ended early, much earlier than usual as he could not rid himself of the guilt that nagged at him, nor keep her compelling face from his mind, and he had returned home after a couple of card games. Losing card games.

"Did you go out?"

"Olivia, I thought we had decided —"

"Decided that we would not interfere with one's lives, yes, that is true," she interrupted him. "However, that does not mean we cannot show interest in one another's activities does it?"

"I am not sure that I feel ... comfortable discussing such things with you."

"Such things as what? Gaming hells and brothels?" she asked without pause.

"Olivia…" he said with a look around him at the servants. The footman, Andrew, seemed to be attempting to hide a smile at his wife's forwardness while his butler frowned with disapproval. "We shall speak of this when we are alone." he lowered his voice, "and I was *not* at a brothel."

"Fine," she said with a shrug, seeming not care, "whatever you say."

He cleared his throat as he drummed his knuckles on the table. What game was she playing? It was certainly not like her to be so agreeable. "And I trust you slept well?"

"Very well, thank you," she responded. "Though it always takes some time to become used to a new bed. Why, I was tossing and turning for hours. Not that I mean to complain, Alastair, for you have very fine sheets, and the mattress —"

"That's very well," he cut her off, gritting his teeth. While a barmaid could not interest him last night, her talk of rolling around on his sheets was causing quite the stir within him. She didn't know what she was doing to him with her words — or did she? Alastair took a closer look at her. Were her lips curled slightly in a smug smile, or was he simply imagining it? He knew she was an innocent, but there was something about the little minx…

"What are you reading?" she interjected into his thoughts.

"Reading? Oh, this," he said, trying to concentrate on her

words as he looked down at the paper in front of him. *"The Financial Register.* There's a new columnist, this P.J. Scott. The man's brilliant. All the gentlemen are talking of him. Anyone who has taken his advice has seen astonishing results. We know not who he is or where he comes from. Perhaps it's an assumed name, as I imagine that should his identity be discovered he would be barraged with more requests than he could possibly handle."

"How very interesting," she said, turning the paper to take a closer look herself. "Have you followed any of his advice?"

"Last year I invested some funds, as he had suggested it was advisable to do so early in one's life. This was before my father passed, and since then I have yet to do anything further," said Alastair with a bit of a sigh as he thought of the state of his finances, and she looked up at him expectantly.

"Is something the matter?"

"Nothing to concern yourself with," he said, masking his face in a smile. "Now, if you will excuse me, I shall be in my study with the steward."

As he exited the room, he passed his sister Anne, who seemed positively delighted to find Olivia awake and at the table. If nothing else, he thought, it was good to have Olivia here as part of Anne's life. Perhaps with each other for company, they both would stay preoccupied and out of any trouble.

He met his steward as pre-arranged in the oppressive study. The dark room was steeped in family history, with paintings and statues that went back decades. It was a constant reminder of the man, who had so strictly dominated them all and yet, in the end, had lacked control over his own state of affairs.

Alastair opened the ledgers and sighed. The facade that his father had created had hidden so much. The former Duke of Breckenridge had been in debt for quite some time and had never deemed to tell him of it. It appeared now that his father had fallen to gambling in his later years, losing a great deal of his fortune. Alastair would never have the opportunity to ask his father what had happened to push him to the tables or the track, but perhaps he had finally grown tired of all his attempts to domineer so much of life that a piece within him had broken. His father must have been careful to avoid Alastair when he was out gambling. Alastair knew his father had visited the odd gentlemen's club, but he had never known the extent to which he spent — and lost. His penchant for the horse track was well known, but it seemed he was rather unlucky when it came to placing his bets.

Now, Alastair was unsure of how they would recover. He had considered a few investments but was concerned he would risk losing even more.

His butler scratched at the door, and Alastair bid him to enter. He set down a tray of brandy on the sideboard before addressing Alastair.

"Your Grace, the steward has been detained," he said. "He shall be along when he has dealt with a matter concerning one of the tenants of Kilpenny."

Alastair nodded, wondering how long it would be until he had a reprieve from the responsibilities hanging over his head. Kilpenny was his country home, and he had been remiss in his attentions to the land he owned there.

As the butler retreated from the room, a blonde head poked around the corner.

"Alastair, I was headed to the library when I overhead Jones. I was wondering if I might come in for a moment?" his wife asked.

Alastair nodded and motioned for her to enter and take a seat in one of the leather wingback chairs in front of the desk he still referred to in his mind as his father's and not his own. He must take a look at redecorating this room, he thought to himself as the scent of jasmine flooded his nostrils as she walked toward the desk.

She gracefully took a seat on the chair that engulfed her and looked up at him with wide blue eyes.

"You seem rather not yourself since we have been married," she began, causing him to frown immediately. What did she know of who his usual self was? "You were always so charming, so talkative, so ... happy, and in the past few days you seem uncharacteristically much less so."

He steepled his fingers together and brought them to his chin, inwardly sighing.

"Previously I did not have a wife to answer to, in case you have forgotten."

"I have not," she said with a bow of her head. "I have considered that it could all be due to my presence, but I believe there is something else causing you melancholy."

He leaned back in his chair, his hands resting on the arms as his gaze wandered over her — the ample bosom he longed to touch again, her delectable curves under her simple lavender muslin morning dress, and her face, open and eager. He sighed. He might as well tell her. After all, she deserved to know what he had planned for her generous dowry, and also what may be awaiting her in the future.

"I am not sure how else to say this but to come directly to the point," he said. "When my father passed, he left my family in significant debt. It seems that he gambled away our entire fortune and more, much on horse racing. Currently many of the gambling establishments in the city are owed money due to his losses. I am trying to determine the best course of action. I am selling a couple of our smaller, less profitable estates, and am determining how much can be fetched on auction by some of the pieces around the house. It will not, however, be enough."

To her credit, she did not react. In fact, she barely blinked as she listened to his words, but maintained her composure and stared at him.

"Did my dowry help at all?"

"I have not touched your dowry," he responded. "I will use that only when it comes to matters of keeping you fed, clothed, and entertained. Basically it is yours to live off of, should I not be able to recover our finances."

"That is generous of you, but not entirely necessary," she said, lowering her eyes before standing and beginning to pace the room. "What of investments?" she asked, surprising him.

"I may take some of this Scott's advice and invest what little I have."

"That would likely be wise," she said, biting the fingernail of her thumb as she paced the room, deep in thought. "Put half into something risky that could allow you to see a good return in little time, and the other half in something more stable but that will grow exponentially."

What in the ... she must have read the column, he thought. But why? He couldn't understand her interest in the subject.

"I appreciate the advice," he said with a droll smile. "I believe I have it handled, however."

She stopped her pacing and looked at him.

"You do not wish for the advice of a woman, is that it?" Her mouth formed a thin line as she crossed her arms, and he was taken aback by how his flippant words had seemingly affected her.

"Not a woman," he said, "but I would prefer the advice of someone with experience in such matters."

"I learned from my father," she said.

"I understand, love, but you have never actually invested, have you?" he asked, looking up at her, trying to explain himself without angering her.

"I have not," she said, though her ire was clearly raised. "If I am so inexperienced, however, then in terms of the investments, perhaps you should contact this Scott person directly," she added, coming to lean over his desk to take a look at the accounts spread out before him.

"That, my dear, is actually quite a splendid idea," he responded, a bit of a grin returning to his countenance as he attempted to remain unaffected by her nearness. "I shall do so immediately."

"And as for the debts to the London establishments..." her eyes gleamed. "I have an idea."

Somehow, he had a feeling that her ideas always led to some sort of trouble, and he was not going to like what next came out of her mouth.

"I will come with you, and win back the money!" she said with some glee. "Oh, what fun it will be. You have seen my skill at whist. If I am able to continue to play the game, I know I shall win, although I believe with practice I could improve in some of the other games as well. It may take some months, but we should be able to clear the debts in due time."

He let her finish, but began shaking his head at her last words. "Olivia, I cannot very well take you into a gaming hell or even back to one of the gambling parties. You are my wife now — a duchess. Never mind the fact that half of the establishments I now owe money to are gentlemen's clubs!"

Her face fell, but her brow quickly furrowed, which he now realized meant she was deep in thought.

"Perhaps, then," she said coyly, sliding a finger along his desktop. "I should go not as myself."

He swallowed at the lushness of her creamy décolletage, overtop the fabric of her dress, that stared him in the face as she leaned over the desk, and he refused to allow her to distract him, though he was not sure whether or not she was purposefully trying to.

"Please do not tell me you are suggesting wearing that awful wig again," he said, shaking his head. "Never mind that, however. These are gentlemen's clubs we are discussing. There is no need for you to be at any sort of gambling establishment. I appreciate your concern, Olivia, but I have it handled. I felt you should know what we are facing, but please do not become overly concerned about it."

"You will find, *darling*, that I am not the swooning or worrying type," she said. "Rather, I prefer to determine how best to solve a dilemma."

"Olivia, leave this alone," he said, raising one eyebrow as if to ensure her acquiescence.

"Very well," she said, the serene smile that so concerned him reappearing on her face. "I trust that you, husband, shall make the best decisions for our future."

And with that she turned and exited the room, leaving him staring after her in bemusement.

CHAPTER 14

Olivia did trust that he would make the best decisions — as well as he could. For what most of society failed to realize was that leaving all of the decisions to men was, in fact, not a wise choice in itself. For it was women who saw how various outcomes affected not only the man, but his wife and family. Or so she believed. She knew she was in the minority, but her opinion would not change. She considered all of this as well as her marriage while she continued down the hallway to the library, the muslin of her skirts rustling with her quick steps.

She was aware she must keep such thoughts to herself. For truly finding your power required more than force, but cunning.

Alastair, however, was slightly different than the typical man. He seemed to somehow see through her smiles and exterior facade. Not that he knew what her plans and opinions were, but rather, that he knew when something wasn't quite right. She could see it in the calculating expression on his face when she glibly responded to something he had said, or the furrow in his brow if she too readily agreed with him. She would have to be careful.

Olivia was pleased with the contents of Alastair's library. It was modest, but the shelves were filled with a fairly wide variety of subjects. He also had subscriptions to many of the journals and newspapers she enjoyed reading, which gladdened her. She had previously read her father's copies, and she had been wondering how to continue to access her daily reading materials.

She picked up copies she had yet to read due to the excitement of the scandal, her wedding, and her move. She made her way over to the chaise lounge, and stretched out across the velvet surface, swinging her legs over the edge.

She tried to concentrate, however her mind kept returning to Alastair's predicament. If only she could help him. She knew she could assist him in making some wise investments; she only wished he would trust her. Perhaps, however, if he did write P.J. Scott, she could write back and he might listen to the advice. It was silly, really, the effort to go through to counsel a person living in the same home, but she would do what she must.

As for the debts owed at the gaming establishments, well … she had plans for that as well.

A smile returned to her face as she thought of what she intended to do. If Alastair wanted to keep from discussing his life with her, that was just fine. However, so too would she.

* * *

OLIVIA GATHERED her latest column and, accompanied by her maid and a footman, set out for *The Financial Register* office on Bond Street. She gave the carriage driver the address for a modiste, conveniently located next door to her intended destination. When she arrived, she told Molly to wait for her in the carriage. The girl protested but Olivia insisted, and she could see the girl's pale face watching her closely through the carriage window as she stepped out and into the brick building.

She smiled at the owner of the dress shop, with whom she had an understanding, before passing through the swirls of white, pastel, and vibrant fabrics into the back corridor of the office, finally emerging outside. She nipped through the alley, knocking on the backdoor of the Register's offices.

"Come in, come in!" Mr. Ungar said with a friendly wave of his hand. He was used to her entrance through the back. She told him her employer was overly cautious about protecting his identity and wanted no one to see her. "I do hope you have another column ready for me, Miss. Your employer's writings are proving to be quite in demand!"

"I am so happy to hear that, Mr. Ungar. Mr. Scott will certainly be pleased. Did he happen to receive any requests from readers this week?" she asked. Often readers wrote in asking Mr. Scott for advice. She enjoyed addressing particular questions in her columns, as she felt if one person had a particular query, perhaps others did as well.

She could not risk anyone discovering her true identity and she had learned from the incident with her mother that she certainly could not accept envelopes delivered to her home, should it be her family home or her new one with Alastair. Therefore the secretary role allowed her to correspond as she pleased without any questions asked.

"I have received requests for Mr. Scott, my dear," the small, rotund balding man replied. "One moment."

He returned shortly with a box of correspondence and shook out the top two papers before handing them to her.

"Here you are," he said. "Nothing particularly interesting.

Basically, where do I invest, how do I plan for the future, how do I regain a lost fortune, and so on."

She took the papers, thanked him, and scurried out to the back alley, eager to determine if Alastair had written, already planning her response.

* * *

DEAR MR. SCOTT, the letter began, and Olivia felt a twinge of an emotion akin to jealousy run through her, although how she was envious of a person who did not truly exist, she wasn't sure. She simply wished her husband would confide in her instead. The letter was not signed, but she had seen enough of Alastair's handwriting to recognize the scrawl.

I have recently inherited a significant amount of debt. I wish to make investments that would allow me to return my estate to financial esteem, while not risk putting myself in further deficit. I would be interested to know your opinion on wise investments for a man in my circumstances.

His question was vague — one that any person with some money to invest would be inclined to ask. She wouldn't normally respond to such a question, but this case was quite obviously different. Olivia had poured over the stocks and selected what she felt were the wisest choices for investments based on their former profit and their future potential. As he wanted to avoid risk, they were potentially profitable, and yet even the riskiest she had selected were fairly safe in her estimation. She wasn't yet sure what amount to recommend that he invest, as she needed to learn more of his actual accounts.

She folded up the letter, determined to respond on the morrow.

That night as she tried to sleep, she tossed and turned,

questioning herself and her advice, as well as the fact she was making it public. She had never before written of actual companies, but had spoken in more generic terms. It kept her awake, as she tried to pry her mind off of the intricacies of what he asked of her, and into the dream world that awaited. It proved a difficult task, however, and Olivia decided to make her way back to the library to write, hoping that by putting her thoughts down on paper immediately instead of waiting until morning, she might be able to go back to sleep.

She lit the candle in the holder and slipped out of her room, pulling the door shut quietly behind her. She tiptoed down the stairs and into the library, where she slowly eased the door open.

Light from the fire still smoldering in the grate cast a shadowy glow about the room, which was otherwise seemingly empty. Olivia found paper and a quill pen from the writing table in the corner, and took it over to the window seat where she could look out over the street below.

She started scratching her thoughts on the paper, which she had placed on top of a book as a writing surface.

"Trouble sleeping?" the voice intruded as she was mid-sentence in her writing, and she jumped with a shriek.

"Shhh," Alastair said with a finger to her lips. "You'll wake Mother and Anne."

"My goodness, Alastair, what in the ... why would you sneak up on me like that? Do you mean to scare out my soul?"

He chuckled, his laugh a deep, throaty vibration in her ear.

"My apologies, love, I did not mean to startle you," he said, squeezing her shoulder and sending tingles down her spine before going to sit in the leather wingback chair across from her. "What are you working on?"

"Nothing of any consequence," she said with a smile. "Simply a list of items I require from my family's home."

He nodded. "Do you miss it?"

"No," she said swiftly, "not the house, anyway. It is horrid, as you noted. I thought I could never miss my mother and her constant nagging, although I feel as if something is now missing in my life without it." She gave a quick laugh. "My sister and I have never been very close, she a quiet mouse and me ... well not as much. My father, however — my father I do miss. He treats me with more respect than most would a daughter. I have always so appreciated that about him." She smiled wistfully.

"You should visit him."

"I shall," she said, "perhaps tomorrow."

She actually did have plans to return home tomorrow, though not, she thought guiltily, to visit her father but rather to gather some items she required to carry out her plans. She did, however, hope he would be home.

"And you?" she asked. "What activities keep you awake at such an hour?"

"I've just returned home," he said, his face flitting between a somewhat rueful grin and a grimace.

"Oh," she said, her own smile faltering. "I suppose I should have gathered that."

"Simply an evening at White's with a few gentlemen," he said, sweeping his hands out as if it were nothing of consequence. "I am sorry, Olivia." Alastair's voice cut through her musings. His tone was quiet, subdued, unlike his usual cheery self.

"Whatever for?" she asked with a raised eyebrow.

"For this. For all of this," he said spanning his hands out in front of him. "For taking advantage of you in a moment of weakness, forcing you into marriage. I know you did not want this."

"Nor did you," she responded with a small, wry smile. "And I believe we both know the role my mother played in orchestrating this match."

He nodded but remained silent, though he raised his eyes from his hands, and the jade green orbs looked into hers with an intensity she had not seen since Lady Sybille's coming-out ball. Her breath caught in her throat.

"Alastair…"

He reached out a hand and trailed a finger down her cheek, coming to rest on her lips before he caught her chin between his fingers. He stood as if mesmerized, and reached down to her, cupping her face between his hands.

She couldn't move. She could hardly breathe as his face inched closer to hers, until he was only an inch away, and she was filled with the scent of sandalwood on his skin and brandy on his breath.

"I am also sorry," he whispered, "for being unable to resist again."

His eyes caught hers, as if waiting for her to draw back, but instead she swiftly closed the distance between them, pressing her lips firmly to his. His mouth moved over hers softly at first, but swiftly growing with a passion unleashed, and she responded by clutching at him as if she were drowning and he was her lifeline to land.

No, she told herself, *no, no, no*. This man was a rake, a charmer who could — and did — seduce any woman he wanted. She was his wife, yes, but she refused to be one of his many conquests. Except … except the feel of his lips on hers, of the way his tongue plundered her mouth, of his hard body pressed up against her, made it far too difficult to push him away. She wanted more of this — wanted more of *him* and the feelings he stirred up within her.

His hands slid down her side, one cupping her bottom as he pulled her closer toward him, so she could feel his desire press into her stomach. She moaned, kneading her fingers into the strong biceps that held her close. She had been kissed before, and she had certainly enjoyed her kiss with Alastair at the ball, but she had never been made love to in this way before. She could feel every ounce of passion flowing through to her, and it was intoxicating.

He bent her backward over the window seat she had been lying upon while writing, stretching himself over top of her as he trailed his fingers lightly from where they cupped her face down her body, over her breasts, to her hip.

As she reached up, moving her hand to run her fingers through his silky blond locks, she heard a crinkle and realized she was rolling over the paper she had been writing on earlier. The paper containing her investment ideas for Alastair — for her husband, the man who didn't trust her, but would take her advice as the financial columnist P.J. Scott.

Her thoughts refocusing, she realized what she was allowing, what she was asking for, and reached up once more, but this time not to pull her husband closer. Instead, she put her hands on his chest and pushed him away. Caught off balance, he fell off of her, landing on the floor with an "oomph".

"Oh, Alastair!"

She slid off the window seat to kneel beside him on the hard wooden floor. "My apologies! I did not mean to … well, I did mean to push you off, but I didn't wish for you to fall."

He gave a slight groan and put his hand to the back of his head, which had bounced off the floor in his surprise.

"I suppose it's my own fault," he said with a slight grimace. "You were fairly clear you didn't want … this. I pushed this on you, Olivia, but damn, why must you be so irresistible to me?"

CHAPTER 15

Her lips, rosy from his kisses, formed a round O, hovering just over his face as she crouched over him in her concern. It was as he had told her — he could not keep himself away from her. When he returned from White's, he had meant to go to his bedchamber and fall into a quick, dreamless sleep. A sleep without thoughts of a golden-haired woman, with a slightly crooked nose and a sly mouth that broke into smile toward him when he did something as simple as pour tea for her in the morning. She haunted his dreams, night and day, and then he had seen her there, sitting in the window seat. The moonlight streaming in through the window highlighted her face, the plait of her hair, and the silhouette of her legs through the thin white material of her nightgown peeking out from beneath her wrapper.

He had been sitting in the overstuffed leather chair in the far corner when he had seen her enter, find the paper, and begin to write. He had meant to leave the library before she noticed him, to return to his bedchamber and leave her to whatever it was that had so captured her attention. Instead, he had made his way over to her, engaging her in a serious conversation that he should not be having with a woman who was determined to keep their relationship simply cordial.

But, oh, how good she had felt under his hands, how soft, how pliant, and how willing to receive his attentions. He had been so taken aback when she pushed him away that he had completely lost his balance and gone tumbling to the floor. The slight bump on his head was worth it, however, to see her overly concerned face so close to his once more.

When she said nothing to his admission of how she drew him to her, he continued to sit up until he was back in a respectable position.

"I am fine, Olivia, truly," he said. "You needn't concern yourself. I offer you my apologies, however. You have been clear in how you feel about our marriage, and I went beyond what you wanted or needed from me."

"That is not —"

"Truly, it is nothing to speak about any longer," he said, rising to his feet and reaching out a hand to help her stand as well. He stood awkwardly for a moment before, knowing not what else to say, he muttered, "Well, goodnight then."

He nodded his head, spun on his heel, and left her standing there gaping after him as he padded over the oriental rug, out the door, and up the stairs to his chambers.

* * *

ALASTAIR REMAINED on his best behavior with Olivia over the next few days. He was polite and charming, but maintained the facade that kept her from realizing the longing he had for her. He wanted to know her body, to make her his wife in more than word, but she had been adamant as to what she expected of their union.

Yes, he had more responsibility now than he had been

HE'S A DUKE, BUT I LOVE HIM

looking for, but despite her words, he found he could not shake the feeling of guilt that followed him from club to club. If he stayed home, however, he would simply be pining for the woman that did not want him. He was caught between two worlds — the bachelor he had been and the married man he was now supposed to be.

Tonight he was to meet Merryweather and a few of his friends, including Lord Penn and Lord Taylor, at a gentlemen's club. It was not as fine as White's nor as seedy as some of the hells, but rather a club for the serious gamblers. His father had been a fan of it, and he was hoping to try to win back some of his debt.

He left the house without saying goodbye to Olivia, as had been his custom since they had married. She was typically ensconced in her rooms or bent over a book in the library and she no longer asked when or where he was going, so he supposed it did not matter to her whether he stayed in or went out.

The hour was later than he had planned to arrive when he entered the club. The tables were full, and the gambling was well underway. He searched the room and did not yet see his friends, so decided to gamble himself until such time they arrived. His gaze happened upon an open space. Whist. A slight smile danced around his lips. Was this not his wife's game rather than his own?

Fine then, he thought with a laugh, he would see if perhaps he had learned anything from her the night they had renewed their acquaintance. How long ago it seemed, and yet how greatly that simple meeting had changed his entire future.

He sat without taking a proper look at the rest of the players, instead focused on the drink in front of him. Each man selected a card to determine first play and pairings, and he began to organize his hand as it was dealt to him.

He surveyed the cards, pursed his lips, and played his chosen card. The second man followed suit. Alastair was continuing to study his own cards when his eyes flicked up to watch the third man make his play.

The hand that reached out was small for a man, the fingers delicate and the nails neatly trimmed. Alastair looked up to take a closer look at the gambler, who was clad in a dark black jacket over a white linen shirt, his cravat neatly tied and a dark hat situated low over his forehead, hiding his face. Then the man looked up to throw his card ... and Alastair froze. They locked eyes, both in complete shock.

"Alastair! Whatever are you doing here?"

"Oliv--"

"Oliver, yes, I'm pleased you remember me! It has been quite some time has it not?" his wife said, quickly recovering her wits as she winked at him — winked at him! — and spoke in a lower tone than her usual alto. He stared back, incredulous. What in the hell was she doing at a gentlemen's club? "I was not aware you would be here this evening, else I ..." she noticed the other players turn to look at her. "I would have looked for you sooner," she finished lamely.

"Why yes," he said slowly, unsure of how to react to her being here. He certainly could not make a scene in the middle of the club, but could he allow his wife to remain? "It would have been interesting indeed to know you would be in attendance tonight. Do you often frequent such establishments?"

"I do like to try my hand at whist when I am able," she responded, "though it has been some time since I have had the opportunity."

The little minx. How long had she been planning an outing such as this? He should have known she was being far too agreeable, too accepting of her new role as mistress of his home. His wife was not a woman who would be content with the domestic duties of most women of her station, that he knew. He almost felt a sense of relief. He had been unsure as to what she had been scheming that had been keeping her attentions occupied. If this was what it had been, well, perhaps it was not so bad.

What he didn't like was the look of her breasts flattened against her chest, presumably by linen or some other sort of material. The jacket was wide in the front, providing her room to move and camouflaging her narrow waist and curves. He saw the need for the subterfuge — this was not a place for women, save for the serving girls. He hoped she at least had the sense to have a footman accompany her to this particular establishment, that she had not come alone. Why was she here, at this club, when there were other places to gamble, such as homes of the *ton*?

The man to Olivia's left turned to whisper something in her ear, and she responded with, "Thank you, Billy, I know," and Alastair felt anger begin to simmer in his belly at the familiarity the man took with her. Who was he, that he knew her well enough to be on a first-name basis? He suddenly realized that he had seen the man before — that night at Lady Atwood's. He had accompanied Olivia home. What did he mean to his wife? He was well-dressed, clearly a man of some means and Olivia certainly seemed to know him well enough to not only accompany him to this club, but give him secrets she had not deemed important enough to share with her husband.

Alastair had been charmed by her play acting, but now his amusement shifted to first annoyance, and then a twinge in his gut. Was this why she wanted nothing to do with him other than their formal marriage arrangement? Did she want another man — love another man? If she could play this game, so could he.

A serving girl came by, offering a tray of drinks to the

gamblers, though from the look she gave him, she would provide him something more, were he interested. He wasn't, but Olivia was not aware of that. He stared back at the woman a moment too long, gifting her with one of his dimpled smiles, before turning back to the table. Olivia was watching. Good. She narrowed her eyes at him, then returned her concentration to the game at hand.

It was fortunate they were partners, for Alastair had completely lost his attention on the cards played, such was he distracted by the ridiculous games he was playing with his wife. However, he could not help himself. He was a man lost and utterly at her mercy.

Somehow they managed to come out ahead by the time the game was over, and Olivia stood up, bid the men thanks, and turned away. Alastair rose to catch her, but her sleek form darted in and out of the crowd, and by the time he found her again, she was already seated at another table, the first hand being dealt. Frustrated, Alastair turned, only to run headlong into a man he well recognized, having spent an entire game of whist staring him down. Olivia's "Billy."

"Your Grace," the man said with a slight bow. "I do not believe I have had the pleasure of your acquaintance. William Elliot."

"William Elliot," he responded, with an arch of his eyebrow. "Please tell me, sir, how are you acquainted with my wife?"

"Ah, the lovely Olivia?" the cad responded with a glint in his eye. "We are childhood friends. We were raised in neighboring estates. My father is the Viscount of Southam and I've only recently returned to town. Olivia needed a partner in her latest adventure and talked me into it."

"Indeed."

It was not a question. Alastair's ire had been raised, and he was not pleased by this turn of events. Why had his wife never mentioned the man? Had there been something between them, perhaps even the promise of a future that was broken by his scandal with her? It would explain much — especially Olivia's desire for a marriage as a simple arrangement in name alone.

He had much to discuss with his wife. And he would do so — tonight.

CHAPTER 16

Olivia was exhilarated. Her plan had been a success. Of course, when she had seen Alastair she had thought it would all be over before it even began, but he had astonished her when he had seemingly gone along with her plan. Although she had to admit if there was a part of the evening that she would choose to forget, it was Alastair's flirtations with the serving women. It was almost as if he had done it on purpose to spite her.

She could hardly believe he had chosen the very same club the exact evening as she. She had decided upon this particular club after careful study. She had to ensure that it was not so exclusive that her presence would be remarked upon, however she preferred to attend a club that had a certain degree of respectability — one where she could gamble without the distraction of sin she could not overlook. She had also spent some time reviewing Alastair's ledgers to determine where his father had created the largest gambling debts.

Her correspondence with William had taken some days to arrange. He had not been particularly pleased with the idea, but had agreed to escort her when she told him she would go with or without him. It had then only been a matter of returning to her family home to gather the men's clothing she had left behind from a previous escapade involving a hunt, and managing to extricate herself from Alastair's house without being seen. Not that she had worried about him discovering her. He was quite uninterested in her whereabouts, or her person in general, with the exception of the few kisses he had stolen when she was apparently conveniently available to him.

She sniffed as William's carriage pulled round the side of Alastair's house as she had instructed the driver. She had departed the club once she had earned the desired amount of money, giving Alastair a quick goodbye before promptly returning home, despite him calling her name into the street as the carriage drove away. She did not want to listen to him lecture her all the way back to the house. She resolved she must fall asleep as soon as possible once she returned home so as to avoid him and also to wake at a respectable hour. She had become used to rising late, but felt she should try her utmost to be early enough to join Anne and greet the Dowager Duchess when she arose. If only, Olivia thought, she was able to fall asleep at night. But alas, every night, as tired as she was, as soon as her head touched the pillow her thoughts began to race and she was awake for many hours.

"It has been an adventure, as always, Olivia," William said, with a nod of his head toward her from where he sat across the seat. "I must tell you, however, I feel your husband may have a few questions for you when he returns. I did tell you that perhaps it was not proper for me to escort you as a married woman."

"Oh Billy, you silly man, none of this is proper!" she said with a laugh. "Why, I am dressed in breeches, so therefore, you did not escort Olivia Finchley, Duchess of Breckenridge, but rather your old friend Oliver. Thank you again, it has simply been the most wonderful evening. Goodnight, darling!"

She alighted from the carriage and slipped in the back door through the kitchens, hopeful she could make it into her bedchamber without notice.

***

Olivia quietly eased open the door to her chambers, opening it only wide enough to fit herself through. The hinges of the heavy oak door creaked if they were pushed too far, and Olivia was thankful that her current attire prevented her from needing any more space to move, such as she did in her typical opulent skirts.

She slipped in and removed her hat and jacket. She was beginning to untie her breeches when a noise came from the corner of the room and she turned, a small shriek escaping her lips before she could keep it in.

"You have already provided me with quite a lot of entertainment this evening, darling, however if you would prefer to continue, pray do so."

"Alastair!" He was in the shadows of her room, his large frame seated on the stool in the corner. The fire in the grate had died to simply embers, and she had not lit a candle so as to escape notice through the halls. "Whatever are you doing?"

"Waiting for you."

"I thought you would still be out."

"I left when you did, however as I rode my horse I arrived quite a great deal quicker than you did with your *friend* William."

"Yes, Alastair, I —"

He stood and walked toward her, coming to stop in front of her. His hands came round her shoulders, and he tilted her head up so their eyes met and held, neither unable to look away for a moment.

"Olivia, darling," he said, surprising her with a softness in his voice instead of anger. "You are my wife now. I know you have this arrangement settled in your mind, but if nothing else, you must allow me to look after you. If you need protection, I will provide it. If you require an escort to a gentlemen's club, come with me. Do not ask another man, please, I beg of you."

She stared back at him in wonderment.

"You would take me to a gentlemen's club? In men's clothing?"

"If that is what you would wish, then so be it. You clearly do not know a great deal about me."

"I suppose not particularly, Your Grace."

"I much prefer Alastair on your lips," he said, releasing his hands from around her. "If you wish to know more about me and my own escapades, perhaps you should ask my mother in the morning. She can provide you with an assortment of stories regarding the mischief I created, and likely the years I have subtracted from her life. Why, my rakish ways are simply a continuation of my childhood."

He winked at her now, mirroring her expression from when they had discovered one another in the club.

"This William character, he says he is your childhood friend," said Alastair, a slight crease now appearing between his brows. "Is this the truth? Or is there something more between the two of you?"

"With William?" her eyes widened. "Oh, good heavens, no. We have always been good friends, yet nothing more. I always saw Billy as a brother, and he felt the same about me."

"I am not quite sure of that," murmured Alastair in such a low tone that she almost did not hear it.

"Well, it is true," she said, stepping back from him, and

lifting the fire poker to try to stoke the embers back to life. "Was there anything else you wished to discuss?"

"What were you doing there, Olivia? Was it a game, or were there potentially greater reasons?"

She sat still for a moment, contemplating how much to tell him. Would he be upset with her? Would he allow her to continue? Tugging off her jacket, which had begun to feel much too warm, she finally determined that the truth, when possible, was typically the best option, and she slowly turned and looked up at him.

"I went there to win back your debt."

The room remained silent but for the cracks of the logs as the fire began returning to life.

"You what?" he finally said, slow and drawn out.

"I determined where your father had amalgamated large amounts of debt, and I chose one of such clubs to win back the money that you now owe."

"You did not think I could do so myself?"

She lowered the fire poker and walked over to him, lifting her hands to his chest so as to soften her words. "You are a good card player, Alastair, but a passable one. Whereas I ... I seem to have the ability to win. In one evening, I made enough to pay back over half your father's debt to that club, Alastair. Is that not wonderful?"

His face was closed off to her as he spoke in a graveled tone. "It is not that I do not appreciate what you have done for me, Olivia," he said. "But it is for me to look after the financial matters, not you."

"That is where you are wrong," she said fiercely, pointing a finger at him. "We are married now, and therefore my finances are yours, and yours are mine. Alastair, I cannot sit in this house day in and day out and do nothing. Let me do this for you — we can do it together if you wish."

He stared at her, his face unmoving. "I shall think on it,"

HE'S A DUKE, BUT I LOVE HIM

he said but then paused. "Although I assume you shall continue no matter what I say."

"Oh Alastair," she said as her face broke out in a wide grin. "You are beginning to understand!"

He laughed then, a chuckle that rumbled deep in his chest, which she could feel through her palms. They began to tingle, sending shots of heat rushing through her arms. She turned and made to step away from him.

"Olivia, you did make one error in calculation," he said.

"What is that?" she asked, turning her head over her shoulder.

"You did not stop to consider what your backside would look like in a pair of breeches," he said with a bit of a growl. With that, he reached out and pulled her against him. She felt his hot breath on her neck before he started to slowly trail kisses down her skin, and she reflexively tilted her head to allow him a better angle.

She couldn't understand how his lips on her neck could cause such feelings to flutter in her stomach and lower, deeper. It left her craving more, and when his hands began to slide down her sides, she grasped them to her, wanting him to put them somewhere, anywhere, and yet she was completely unaware of where that should be. He seemed to know, however.

His fingers moved up her body, leaving a line of fire where they lingered, before coming to her breasts. He made to cup her, but cursed when he felt only the swath of linen that was tied tightly around her. He unbuttoned the shirt, slipped it off her shoulders and grasped an edge of the fabric binding her, slowly unwinding it from her body. She felt the material begin to release, allowing her to breathe deeper and also providing room for his hands to reach in and flick over the rosy bud of her nipple. She arched back into him and could feel his desire pressing into her, just overtop the swell of her behind.

His hands reached down to her waist then, turning her so she was facing him. His mouth took hers then, and he kissed her long and hard, drinking her in, before his mouth ripped away from hers. She cried out for him to return to her lips, but then accepted their absence when he began to lick at her nipple, while attending to the left side with his thumb and finger. She moaned, unable to keep herself from responding to him and his practiced caresses.

"Olivia, love," he said between jagged breaths. "Do you want this? You must say no now, or I'm unsure if I will be able to stop myself."

"Yes," she breathed out, "yes, I want this. Don't stop."

He picked her up, spreading her legs, still clad in the breeches, wide around him as he carried her back to the bed. He deposited her upon it before ripping off his own shirt and climbing onto the mattress, straddling her. Before he could do anything further, Olivia reached up and began to unlace his own breeches with trembling fingers. She wanted — no, she needed — to see more of him and she could no longer wait. He let her do so, watching her face as she bit her lip in concentration. Her gaze caught his as she looked up at him, but she refocused back on her task, her eyes widening when he sprang free.

"You..." she swallowed, "you are very large."

He chuckled his deep throaty laugh and kissed her mouth gently. "Have no fear, love, you'll be ready for me."

He repaid her favor in kind, untying her own breeches before peeling them off and throwing them from the bed. This was lovely, she thought, to have so few layers of clothing. It had taken no time at all for Alastair to undress her. Her thoughts soon became addled, however, as his fingers began brushing their way down her stomach, lower, until they —

"What are you doing?" she asked, gasping as he skimmed the pad of his thumb against her nub in her most tender, private area.

"I'm preparing you," he said, "and teaching you of pleasure. You may best me at cards, love, but this I will teach you."

He slipped one finger, then two inside her, and she thought she was nearly ready to come apart, such was the depth of feeling within her. She craved something more, to reach the pinnacle of something that was just out of her grasp.

"Are you ready, love?" came Alastair's voice in her ear. It was all she could do to nod, before she felt the heaviness of him beginning to enter her. "Steady," he said, as he paused for a moment before breaking through. She expected pain — her mother had told her much of it — but it was nothing much, really, and what hurt more than anything was Alastair's pause. When she began to move, he slowly matched her rhythm, until he was pistoning his hips in and out of her in a way that felt, oh, so good. She finally went over the edge, his name on her lips, as the world shattered around her.

CHAPTER 17

Alastair woke the next morning with his wife in his arms, feeling completely and utterly content. Who would have believed this day would ever come, he thought with a laugh. Alastair Finchley, married, and surprisingly happy about it. He looked down at the woman next to him. Her golden hair fanned out behind her, glistening in the sunlight that streamed through the window. Her long eyelashes rested against the soft skin of her face, as she looked entirely peaceful and at ease. She was always so animated, so fiery, that he took advantage of the opportunity to study her while she slept.

She had been more passionate than any woman he had ever met before. She approached their lovemaking as she did everything in life, with a zeal unlike any other. He hadn't meant to make love to her last night; he had only wanted to speak to her about the evening and the man who had accompanied her. But he had found his thoughts dissolving into nothing but a wanting for her — her body, her mind, and her spirit.

She stirred, as if feeling his eyes on her, and slowly

opened her lids to reveal sleepy crystal-blue eyes, that warmed when they took in his face above hers.

"Alastair," she said with a slight grin, and he nearly wanted to take her again right there, but knew it may be ill advised to do so.

"Did you sleep well, love?" he asked, returning her smile.

"I actually slept better than I have in months," she responded, seeming somewhat surprised. "It has been quite some time since I have fallen — and remained — asleep without any issue."

"Well I am sure that had all to do with the strong arms of your protector around you," he said with a grin, then ducked as she swatted him with a pillow. "I jest, Madame," he said. "As we both are well aware, you are more than capable of caring for yourself."

"Ah, Alastair, you do not realize how wonderful it is to hear you say such," she said, pushing herself up to a sitting position, though he didn't miss how she pulled the bed linen up to cover herself. She looked up at him then, her eyes slightly troubled.

"Thank you for maintaining my charade at the gambling establishment," she said. "Why were you willing to allow me to stay when so many men would not?"

He shrugged. "You are a grown woman, Olivia. While you may be my wife, you were very clear on your view of our marriage. You have said nothing as I have left our home time and again come the evening; therefore, what right do I have to prevent your actions?"

"Were I discovered, I would have brought great shame to your family," she said, feelings of guilt and yet exhilaration at war within her.

"Then we are fortunate that no one was the wiser," he said. "You have much to learn about me, however, love. I am not a stranger to outrageous acts. Do you plan to do the same again?"

She hesitated. "I would like to, however, I understand if you feel I am not in a position to do so."

He looked up at her, mischief in his eyes. "I must tell you, love, that you are currently in the best position possible — underneath me."

She gasped, then laughed as he — very gently — showed her once again the pleasures lovemaking could offer.

* * *

Alastair was true to his word and accompanied Olivia to a great many events over the next fortnight. They attended some balls and soirees as husband and wife, where they were spoken to by a great many guests, many less than subtly interested in learning more about their relationship and the scandal that had caused it. Other nights, they attended gambling houses and establishments. Sometimes Olivia dressed as Mrs. Harris, pretending she had no connection to Alastair, and the odd time dressed in her breeches and introduced as Alastair's cousin, Oliver. They developed a system for whist and easily won money each game. Alastair's gambling debts were slowly ebbing away, and he had his wife to thank completely. He was unsure of how he felt regarding the subject. On the one hand, he was proud of her intelligence. He appreciated the way in which she drew people to her, much in the same way he enjoyed a crowd, and her quick wit and easy laugh was contagious. On the other, he felt he wasn't quite the man he should be, needing his wife to help.

And every time she donned a pair of those breeches ... they were equally as enticing as the swell of her bosom over the low-cut neckline of her dress. He was enjoying teaching her the art of lovemaking, and she was certainly a willing student.

They had finished dining one evening, his mother having retired, and were sitting near one another on the sofa of the drawing room as Anne played the pianoforte, the lively, tinkling melody dancing around their ears.

"We have no engagements this evening. Are you leaving the house?" she asked.

"Just to White's," he said nonchalantly. "'Tis nothing of import. Make a few wagers, have a couple of drinks, and I should be home in due time."

"Alastair…" she said, staring down at her hands before her brilliant blue eyes rose to meet his, her lips spreading into a smile that made him both excited and on edge at the same time. It was the look that told him she wanted something and expected him to help her to get it.

"Yes, darling?" he said.

"Would you take me to White's?"

His eyes nearly bugged out of his head. "To White's? White's Gentlemen's Club where no woman enters — ever?"

"Yes!" she said, her eyes shining. "Would it not be a thrill? To enter undetected?"

"And if we are found out?" he asked. "If someone were to recognize you? I would be disbarred from White's for life, as would any heirs of mine!"

Her face fell slightly as she reconsidered her request and the potential consequences. "All right then," she finally said with a shrug. "It's no matter."

He eyed her. Did she mean that, or would she attempt to enter herself? He could tell she was disappointed, but he knew it was for the best. There was no way he should take her to White's, let alone any gentlemen's club.

"Fine, I shall take you."

The words came out of his mouth hardly before he realized what he was saying. What was he agreeing to? Did he truly so badly wish to keep her happy that he would take her to a place like White's?

"Oh, splendid!" she said, her face coming to life and he forgot his misgivings in the moment. "Excellent. When shall we leave?"

* * *

He had seen her dressed as a man before, but she seemed to becoming more adept at it each time. Tonight, she had taken extra care to bulk up her body, completely hide the color and length of her hair, and had darkened her eyebrows considerably. The brilliant blue of her eyes still shone, however, and her shapely legs were once again apparent through the breeches. "Though," she told him when he remarked upon them, "I shall be sitting down the majority of the time, so no one will notice."

He was skeptical at that. He certainly noticed.

She was near trembling with excitement in the carriage as they traveled to the club. He, who was seldom affected by any matter, could barely speak to her, his nerves were so on edge. It was one thing to have a bit of fun sneaking into a gambling establishment or a lady of the *ton*'s home, but White's? It was the most prestigious club in London. They would have no qualms about turning away a duke for doing something as untoward as bringing a woman into their ranks. What had he been thinking, agreeing to this?

He resolved when — if — they managed to enter, he would simply ensure she had a quick look at the place, and then he would escort her out as quickly as he could manage.

"Olivia," he said, taking her hands in his so that she would pay attention to him. "I have a few rules for you tonight."

"You mean to set boundaries upon me?" she asked.

"You are aware of what you have asked me to do this evening?"

Her face softened. "Yes, and I do appreciate it, Alastair. What are your requests?"

He smiled, not missing her choice of words. "Should you see men you know, you will not converse with them, but rather avoid them at all costs so you are not recognized. You will keep to yourself and not make any type of scene. And you will never — ever — tell anyone of this. Not Rosalind, not Isabella — no one. Understood?"

She tilted her head to the side as she studied him for a moment, suddenly realizing just how upset he was by this plan of hers.

"Alastair, we do not have to go," she said quietly. "I believe I didn't quite realize just how important your membership is to you. Perhaps we should not risk it for this foolhardy idea of mine."

"We've come this far," he said with a shrug. "Why not go ahead now?"

The rest of the carriage ride was fairly silent until they neared St. James's Street, and Olivia began reviewing their cover story, which Alastair realized was for her own benefit as well as his. As they walked up to the white Portland stone building, he had to resist the urge and the familiarity of taking her arm.

"Good evening, Your Grace," the man at the door greeted Alastair. "Welcome to White's this fine evening. Have you a guest?"

"I do," responded Alastair. "My cousin, Oliver Harris, is visiting from Bath and shall be joining us this evening."

"Very good, Your Grace," the man said, allowing them entrance.

Glancing at Olivia, she seemed immediately enthralled by the club as he led her on a quick tour of the morning room, the smoking room, and finally the billiards room. "It looks very much like the rooms of a man of the nobility," she said to him, and he nodded in return. A quick look around, he told himself, then they would be out the door and back home. He turned to ask what further she needed to see when he heard his name being called and he cringed.

"Breckenridge!" He turned to find Lord Penn and Lord Merryweather beckon him.

"Stay here," he said to Olivia. "Merryweather knows you well enough, he will likely recognize you."

"I shall stay in the shadows," she promised, "and I shall not say a word."

He looked around for an escape, but seeing no other option than leaving her on her own, which would never do, he turned and walked toward his friends, taking the seat closest to them so that Olivia would be hidden in the darkness of the corner. Alastair was grateful for the low light of the room, the wall sconces and wax candles lit at intervals, providing a comfortable feel.

"Gentlemen," he said as he joined. "I am accompanied tonight by my cousin, who surprised us all with a visit. Mr. Oliver Harris, Lord Penn and Lord Merryweather."

They exchanged pleasantries and called for a round of brandies before Penn began to question him.

"Breckenridge, man, how do you find marriage is keeping you these days?" he asked.

"Well, thank you," responded Alastair cautiously.

"You never did tell us the details of the scandal leading to your wedded bliss. I should be quite intrigued to hear more of it."

Alastair cleared his throat. "A small misunderstanding is all."

Penn chortled. "A small misunderstanding. Surely you jest. Breckenridge, you sat here but not a few weeks prior to your blessed event telling us you wanted nothing to do with a wife for years to come. 'Responsibility and guilt,' I believe were the words you used, were they not?"

"Ah ... I am not sure those were quite the words I used," he said, trying to determine how best to change the subject. "I say, Penn, tell me of Tattersalls last week — how did you fare?"

As Lord Penn began rambling about his latest horse gamble, Alastair leaned back in his chair. This was not a good start to the evening. Could it get any worse?

CHAPTER 18

Responsibility and guilt? That was what marriage meant to the man? Olivia's eyes narrowed as she took in Alastair and his friends. Fools, all. She was no one's responsibility, particularly not Alastair Finchley's.

She yearned to provide these men with her opinion, but knew there was too much at risk to speak, which would draw attention to herself and possibly give away her true identity. Instead, she sat there and fumed in silence, narrowing her gaze at Alastair, who clearly felt the ire of her glare as he fidgeted in his seat.

Besides the ridiculous conversation, she did all she could to take the opportunity to enjoy her foray into White's. She wondered how many women had done this before, snuck into the club that was completely off limits to them. Perhaps a women-only club was in order, what would men say to that?

Olivia did have to admit that she enjoyed the comfortable masculinity of the decor. The chairs were rich chestnut leather, the walls lined in shelves of books and rich wallpaper.

"How fares your sister, Breckenridge?" asked Merryweather, and Olivia's head swiveled to take a closer look at him. He was a handsome gentleman, dark haired with warm brown eyes and a pleasant enough countenance.

"Anne is fine, thank you for asking, Merryweather," Alastair responded with some heat in his tone.

"I am sorry to see she has not yet resumed her season following your father's death, though of course the circumstances are understandable," said Merryweather. "You must ensure I am invited to her first engagements."

"Oh yes," countered Alastair, "I will take a close look at the guest list, I assure you."

Interesting, thought Olivia. Lord Merryweather was interested in Anne. She wondered if Anne felt anything toward him, or even knew much at all of him. She had certainly never mentioned him to Olivia. She would have to ask Alastair more about his friend. He did not look to be a bad sort at all.

"And have you seen the lovely Baroness of Hastings since the joyous occasion of your marriage?" asked Penn. The conversation had returned to Alastair's married life.

She could feel heat rising in her own cheeks as her sharp gaze flew to Alastair's face.

It would not have been physically possible for him to look more uncomfortable. Were she not so disturbed by the question, she would have found it rather amusing.

"I have not," he said, lifting his drink to his lips, apparently resolved to say no more on the subject.

"Ah, the poor woman will be lonely, will she not?" asked Penn. "Are you sure you would like to give up the boundless energy of the woman from your bed?"

"Of course, Penn," he replied. "I am married now."

"Ha!" Penn barked in laughter. "When has that kept a man from bedding his beautiful mistress? I say, Breckenridge, I am not sure what ails you this evening, but you are certainly not your usual self. We must have another round of drinks, perhaps that will better your countenance."

Penn ordered another round of brandies for the four of them. Olivia tossed hers back nearly as fast as Alastair, who then rose to his feet. "I am afraid we must be off. We have another engagement and simply stopped in for a drink. Good evening, gentlemen."

Not yet ready to leave, but not seeing any way to protest in front of Alastair's friends, Olivia nodded at them, then scurried behind him lest he lose her on his rushed exit out the door.

Olivia said nothing until the carriage came round, and once again had to keep Alastair from naturally helping her inside. They sat inside, across from one another. She crossed her legs, enjoying the freedom of the breeches, and removed her hat, shaking her hair out so that it spilled around her shoulders.

He cleared his throat. "Olivia..."

"Responsibility and guilt?" she asked, her eyebrows raised high.

"Well, you see, that was before —"

"The Baroness of Hastings?"

"Once again, that was before —"

"*Boundless energy* in your bed?"

Her initial teasing tone had somewhat darkened now as she threw the words back at him.

"Olivia," he leaned forward. "This was your idea, to come here tonight."

"I know," she said with a sigh.

"Do not young women speak to one another of the men in their lives?"

"What young women speak of is nothing at all like the conversation I heard in there!" she responded, throwing her arms wide. "Although … it would be rather nice to speak so openly without fear of scandal or retribution. I do realize it is my own fault to have heard such things, Alastair, although I must admit that it still somewhat pains me to realize how our marriage has so adversely affected you, and that you might prefer other … things."

"Other women you mean?"

Her cheeks flamed. "Yes."

"Olivia," he said, moving with the rocking of the carriage over the cobblestone streets to sit beside her and take her hand in his, which she some reluctantly allowed. "Those men spoke of my past. My thoughts on marriage were different then. I did not expect to marry such an … interesting … woman. I cannot lie that I do feel responsibility to your well-being, and I do feel guilt when I am out and have left you at home, however it cannot be helped. There are certainly more positives aspects to our marriage than I would have thought possible. As for women in my bed, it matters not who came before you, for now you are my wife, and the only woman I want beside me. And, if you would like to know, I have known no enthusiasm like yours ever before."

Somewhat mollified, she squeezed his fingers. She could not deny that she was still upset, that a part of her did not want to forgive him and would rather harden her heart against his words. But the rational part of her mind could not deny what he said held truth. He could not change the past. She knew it when she married him, and he could not control the words of his friends.

She finally forced a smile and said, "I understand, Alastair. Perhaps my foray into White's Gentlemen's Club has satisfied my curiosity for now."

He sighed in relief as he fell back against the squabs. "Thank God," he said, "for I do not think I could do that once more."

She laughed, and all seemed forgiven.

* * *

Alastair's days continued to be spent primarily tending to his estate and his finances, trying to determine the best way forward to begin to make a profit once more. He was in his study pouring over the ledgers when the butler came to the door with his correspondence.

"For you, Your Grace," he said before exiting once more.

Alastair shifted through the notes, finding two of interest. He picked up his letter opener to tear them each open and quickly read through, a mix of emotions coursing through him. One letter seemed to hold his demise, the other the key to his recovery. He was contemplating his next course of action when he sensed a presence in the room and looked up to see his wife enter.

"Is all well?" she asked. "You seem quite surprised."

"Yes, indeed," he replied. "Would you like to sit down?"

She sat cautiously, looking concerned.

"The first letter has noted that many of my father's debts have come due," he explained. "I have but a month to pay them back."

She held out a hand for the letter, which he reluctantly passed over to her.

"Do you suppose you could arrange with them to pay the debt back in installments?"

"Perhaps," he said, inclining his head to her. "Fortunately, it is not all dire news. You recall the financial columnist I spoke to you about?"

"I do."

"It seems instead of addressing my concerns in the Register, he instead wrote me back with his suggestions. That is quite odd, is it not?"

She tilted her head to the side. "Perhaps he felt he could not provide the same advice to all readers or there would become difficulty with investments. What did he say?"

He cleared his throat and read.

"'Your Grace, the Duke of Breckenridge. I am humbled that you would write to ask for my advice on your investment matters. I cannot provide you with certainty that my recommendations shall prove profitable; however, upon further study I believe the following to most likely benefit you financially.' Then he lists various investments he has deemed both secure and potentially rewarding, suggesting I invest funds in some of various nature."

He continued to look at the letter, looking contemplative.

"It seems understandable that he would write you back directly. For it would not do to provide all investors with the same advice. It sounds very promising!" Olivia said with a cheery grin. "In what do you suppose you shall invest?"

"Pardon me?"

"Which investments shall you choose?"

"Ah, Olivia," Alastair said, folding the paper in front of him. "My apologies, love, for droning on so. I imagine you cannot possibly be interested in all this talk of finance and investment."

"Why ever not?" she asked, a furrow coming to her brow.

"As I can hardly stand to think of such things, I cannot see how you would be interested," he said with a wave of his hand. He was shocked when she reached out and also took this paper from the desk in front of him.

"Hmm..." she murmured, her eyes skimming the words on the page. "It seems the shipping company could perhaps be worth pursuing, does it not? And the fund is interesting, but perhaps does not offer a great return quickly enough, does it? Invest in a bit of both perhaps?"

Heaven help him. He knew she was trying to be helpful,

but to pick names off of a list because she liked the sound of one over the other certainly was not going to be of any aid.

"Thank you, dear," he said, sending what he hoped was a benevolent smile her way. "However, please do not concern yourself with such affairs. I should not even have mentioned such things to you. You must know, your settlement will more than cover any needs that will arise for you should anything happen to me. Now, darling, what do you say we attend the theatre this evening? We have been invited by Lord and Lady Greville. I believe you will enjoy their company."

Olivia stood with a polite smile on her lips and gave him a frosty, "Whatever you would like, Your Grace," before departing with a swirl of her skirts. "I am sorry you regret sharing your *concerns* with me." He cursed under his breath. He did not know what he had done to invoke her ire, but he certainly had, in spades.

* * *

OLIVIA FUMED as she dressed for the evening to attend the bloody concert. Not concern herself in such affairs. Did he really believe her to be so simple minded that she would not have a valid opinion on his investments? What he chose would have great effects on the two of them and their future. Though she supposed, if she stopped to think on the subject, he was right in that most women simply would not care at all.

She resolved that this would not be the case with their marriage. It would be a partnership regarding such matters as business. She simply had to find a way to encourage him to listen to her and entertain her thoughts.

In the meantime, she would prepare for the theatre. She was unsure what they were to take in this evening, but she hoped it was something ripe with both comedy and drama, that would capture and keep her attention. She called for Molly and set out to provide the housekeeper with information regarding the evening's plans for supper. She did not know Lord and Lady Greville well, but Olivia resolved to do her best to enjoy the evening, despite her frustration with Alastair and his simple-minded views on what she would consider important.

Her maid chose a deep-purple silk for her to wear that evening, which Olivia approved of with a nod. It was beautiful, more vibrant than was the current style, but she had always enjoyed it, as it was the perfect complement to the rich blonde tones of her hair. Her maid lifted a delicate gold chain and showed it to Olivia with a question in her eyes. Olivia nodded, and turned to allow her to close the clasp of the necklace, as the small charm came to rest on her chest between her collarbones.

Meanwhile, she could not stop her thoughts from racing. She hoped Alastair would write back P.J. Scott. It was the only way she could make him listen.

CHAPTER 19

The play was, unfortunately as Olivia had expected, exceptionally boring. She hadn't realized her eyes had drifted shut until Alastair nudged her in the side. How was it that she found sleep so elusive in a luxurious bed through the night, yet she could nod off in the middle of a theatre hall with all matter of instruments playing and people shouting at one another? Although, if she were to be honest, she had been sleeping quite well lately with Alastair by her side, although she would never admit to him the effect he was having on her.

Perhaps it was the warm body next to her. Perhaps it was the satiety he brought her before they slept. Or perhaps — and she could hardly admit it to herself — he did bring a sense of comfort and security that she had not felt before.

Alastair had been correct regarding Lord and Lady Greville. She did enjoy their company. Lady Greville was extremely pleasant and intelligent, and quite interesting to converse with.

Through intermission she was speaking with her about mutual acquaintances when she overheard Alastair asking

HE'S A DUKE, BUT I LOVE HIM

Lord Greville for his advice — on investments. Her head whipped around. He would not discuss the matter with her, and yet had no qualms of discussing with a friend? Her mouth worked. She should say nothing — it was not her place. And yet ... Olivia was never one to stay silent. It was a trait that had nearly earned her spinster status, that had plagued her mother for years.

"I believe shipping is always a safe bet," Lord Greville was saying. "Particularly with the East Indian Company continuing to grow, as well as rising interest in travel to the Americas. If I were to place funds in an investment, I should say that would be my choice."

"Why, Alastair, darling," Olivia said with a sweet, practiced smile, "was that not what I was suggesting just this morning?"

Lord Greville's eyebrows shot up, and he gave her a slight nod as Alastair turned to look at her with a perplexing expression.

"You did," he acknowledged. "Did it not simply sound like an exciting opportunity to you? I know of your love of adventure."

She snorted, causing Lady Greville to let out a bit of a chuckle. Olivia thought she saw a look of respect in the woman's eye, however it could have simply been her imagination.

"Surely you do not believe I would suggest you invest funds into a company solely based on the activities of said business? Do you think me a simpleton?" she asked, her ire growing at his complete lack of recognition of any sort of intellect. "Come, now, Alastair, have more sense than that."

His usual easygoing countenance shifted somewhat as he began to look slightly uncomfortable. "My apologies, darling," he said in his attempt to keep peace in front of his friends. "We shall discuss this at greater length in due time.

Now tell me, Lady Greville, how fares your father? I know he and my own father were well acquainted, and I have not seen him in some time."

"Quite well, thank you, Your Grace," she said with a smile, and while the conversation lightened and continued, Olivia could not help but feel like a chastised child, and when they resumed their seats she could feel the frosty chill settle between she and her husband.

* * *

ALASTAIR COULD NOT UNDERSTAND what had come over his wife. Why was she suddenly so interested in financial matters? Although, come to think of it, perhaps he simply did not yet know her well enough to have a grasp of what she *was* interested in. She certainly did not seem to take up any of the usual hobbies of a young titled lady, such as watercolors or embroidery or anything of the sort. Rather, she spent most of her time in the library, her head in books or journals, or busy scribbling away on her paper. She was certainly well learned, but he had never thought to ask what it was she was so focused on. Instead, he had always supposed that she would keep to her business and he to his own.

They bid goodnight to Lord and Lady Greville, and continued on their way out of the theatre to find their carriage. He turned to speak to Olivia when he felt a hand run down his arm.

"Alastair! Oh, my apologies, I should say Your Grace, I suppose, as we no longer have the relationship we once did, do we darling?" As the words slid off the women's ruby lips, she pressed her ample bosom, which was practically spilling out of her dress, into his arm. He cringed. He did not see how this encounter could end in any way other than disaster.

HE'S A DUKE, BUT I LOVE HIM

"Oh, and who is this lovely creature? Perhaps the reason for your absence? You *must* introduce me."

"Olivia," he said, turning to his wife, who was eyeing the woman with thinly veiled contempt, her gaze focused on where the woman still clung to his other side. "May I introduce you to the Countess of Oxbridge, Georgina Porter. Countess, this is my wife, Olivia Finchley, the Duchess of Breckenridge."

The woman gave a peal of laughter. "Oh Alastair, I heard that you had married, but I never believed it to be true! Why, she is simply divine. You are most beautiful, Your Grace, although I am sure you must know that. Whatever did you do to convince him to marry you? I had thought him a confirmed bachelor for life!"

Alastair's cheeks grew hot as he risked a sideways glance at his wife, who seemed to stand taller as she wore the smile that he had come to recognize as danger despite how innocent it seemed.

"Olivia is an intriguing woman, Countess," he said demurely. "Once she caught my attention, I simply could not imagine life without her."

"Thank you, darling," Olivia said, casting that smile upon him, causing him to shiver. "How lovely to make your acquaintance, Countess. Tell me, how do you happen to know my husband?"

Alastair gave a bit of a choke as he prayed the woman would not divulge their former relationship at this point in time. Unfortunately, God seemed unwilling to answer his prayers.

"Oh," the Countess said, toying with one of her dark ringlets as she looked up at Alastair. "We met through society functions, I suppose, and found that we quite enjoyed one another's company from time to time, did we not, Your Grace? Though I have not had the pleasure of a visit from you in the past couple of months, I'm afraid. Now I see why. How wonderful, as I thought you had simply tired of me!"

Alastair inwardly groaned as he attempted to extricate himself from the conversation.

"Yes, well, I must admit, we have been rather busy since our marriage," he said hurriedly. "Oh! See here, our carriage has arrived. Goodnight, Countess."

As they settled themselves on the plush seats of his carriage, he leaned his head back against the squabs and closed his eyes. Perhaps she would think nothing of the encounter, he thought. Or perhaps she would say nothing. Perhaps she would not care….

"How long was the Countess your paramour?"

Perhaps he was wrong.

He opened his eyes, blinking as if he misunderstood her.

"Pardon me?"

"I asked you," she said slowly, as if he were simple minded, "for how long was the Countess your lover."

Her face was stoic, not betraying any of the emotion that he was sure was simmering under the surface. He was beginning to see why some men preferred to have wives without the intelligence of his, who were content to spend their days focused on the latest fashions and gossip of the day, caring not of their husband's business or even who they took to bed. He sighed.

"Now and again for a few years," he said, too much of a coward to meet her eyes. "There was no relationship, nothing consistent. She was a widow, and wanted some fun now and again. I was always up for a bit of it. But, Olivia, we have discussed this before. She is simply part of my past, as you well know, and I hold no feelings toward her."

She nodded, not betraying any of what she was feeling, saying nothing as she stared out the window. While he understood her displeasure in the encounter with the Countess, she must understand that while their marriage meant he would no longer take a lover, there may be instances when such women would engage him in conversation. He knew, however, that now was not the time to tell her of this. Alastair did not enjoy conflict and was usually quite adept at easing difficult conversations into lighter territory. However, Olivia saw beyond his flippant words and attempts to mask deeper emotions, leaving him in a place of unease, as he did not know how to address her. He felt he would rather she shout at him, to provide him with an understanding of her thoughts so he might know how best to respond. Instead, she simply sat there, and he felt his words were simply sending him into greater peril.

"Olivia?" he questioned. "There may be times when women such as the Countess approach me, but I promise you that I will never act upon any such overtures. You must understand —"

"I understand perfectly," she said, still wearing the smile that he longed to lean over and erase with a kiss that would show her she was the only one he currently desired to warm his bed. "From when we met, I have always understood who you were. You cannot change your past and I understood that. However, I allowed myself to be swept away by your charm and your caresses, to the point that I somehow lost sight of the fact that you are a man that woman love to love, Alastair. Do you truly see yourself with only one woman for the rest of your life?"

"I — of course I do," he said, but not without a moment of hesitancy that he immediately cursed. "I am married to you now, and I will not betray you."

"That may be true, but is that what you want?" she asked, her smile now turning genuinely sad. "Do you want a life in which you feel tied to me out of a sense of honor and duty? I will not hold you to that. I will be no one's responsibility, I will not keep you away from what you want most of life. I will not be a duty, nor an obligation. Answer me honestly, Alastair, am I all you want, for the rest of your life?"

"When I married you, I understood it was to forsake others," he said truthfully, to which she gave a bark of laughter and looked away from him back out the window.

"As I thought, Alastair," she said softly, and the unshed tears swimming in her eyes tore at his heart. "As I thought."

* * *

OLIVIA DISMISSED her maid for the evening, and sat on the stool in front of the ornate oval mirror, taking a close look at her reflection. She picked up her brush and began to slowly run it through her long blonde hair, which waved loosely about her shoulders. It was therapeutic, and she closed her eyes as she willed away the thoughts that tore round her head. When she had seen the woman approach Alastair, she knew instantly who she was, who she had been to her husband. Olivia knew she had no right to be angry, was in no position to make any demands on her husband more than what he had given her, had promised her. Yet she could not help the feelings of jealousy and hurt that tore through her and, to be honest, she felt a fool. How many women were there, who would continue to haunt them? Did others laugh at her and her apparent naivety regarding her marriage?

She did not want him to be with her simply because he felt beholden to his vows. She did not want him to live a life of regret over what might have been. And she did not want to be relegated to this foolishness into which she had allowed her emotions to draw her.

She heard the opening of the door which connected their chambers, the footfalls of his boots as he crossed the room toward her. She kept her eyes closed as his hands came about her and gently eased the hairbrush out of her grasp. He began to slowly trail the brush over her hair, picking up where she had left off. As the bristles swept through the strands of her blonde waves, it brought a peaceful calm over her, and she leaned back into him, despite the thoughts that swirled through her mind.

"I must apologize, Alastair," she finally said, breaking the quiet. "I was not fair to you. As you said, your past cannot be helped, but it is painful to be looked upon as a fool by these women."

"No, it cannot be helped," he responded quietly. "Though I do apologize at the awkwardness of the encounter and I shall do my very best to shield you from any in the future."

She nodded but said nothing. She had known, when she first entered the private box with this man, what it would mean to give her heart to him. He was a man who had the potential to not only break it, but shatter it. He would be easy to love, but she would not allow herself to give him that piece of her, for she would then also be giving him the power to utterly crush her. It was why she had initially resisted going to bed with him, though her desire had eventually overcome her stubborn unwillingness to give in.

All she could now do was keep the shield around her heart very strong. She had given him her body, but resolved to never give her heart — or her soul. For him to tear them apart would be her undoing.

CHAPTER 20

Alastair hummed a tune as he made his way down the corridor between his study and the library a few days later. Tonight he and Olivia had been invited to a ball at the home of the Duke and Duchess of Stowe. They had accepted, as they did most invitations. He and his wife were both social beings, it was true, but the feeling of unease that had entered their relationship the night of the theatre had retained its hold on them. While they maintained a cordial relationship and a sharing of the marital bed, he could feel the walls she had raised around her, as it seemed she was keeping him at a distance.

In truth, he was not sure what to make of his wife. He enjoyed her company, both her quick wit as well as the passion she injected into everything she did, be it planning a dinner menu or entering into a conversation regarding any number of subjects. Yet he felt his own reluctance to truly give his heart over to her. For so long his entire life had been a series of entertainments, from balls to gambling halls to even the odd brothel. To give himself wholly to his marriage seemed to be saying goodbye to the man he had once been.

HE'S A DUKE, BUT I LOVE HIM

Their late night adventures had also come to a halt since the disastrous visit to White's. She had not suggested any further, and nor had he. Their shared mischievous outings had pulled them together as co-conspirators, and now it seemed neither wished to take the step back together in such a way.

He had not, however, gone out alone either. He had forgone doing so when he realized she wished to accompany him, and now it seemed that to go without her would somehow be a betrayal. He sighed. This was why he had chosen to remain a bachelor — so that these confounded conflicts would have no bearing upon him. A married man he was now, however, so he supposed he would have to deal with it as best as he was able.

Perhaps tonight, when they returned home from the ball, which was sure to put them in good spirits, they could have another go-round discussion about their life together and what was expected from each of them. He couldn't change the past, but if she would at least tell him what he needed to do to return their relationship to the one he loved, the one of friendly banter, knowing smiles, and spirited lovemaking, it would be quite preferable.

He rounded the corner to the library, spotting Olivia perched on the window seat that had become hers, to his way of thinking. She hadn't heard him, so engrossed she was in her work. She was scribbling madly, messily, and he had such an urge to know what it was that had so captured her attention.

He walked up behind her, not wanting to startle her but also not wanting to call her attention away when she was so focused.

"Olivia?" he said, question in his voice.

"Alastair!" she all but jumped off the window seat. "I had no idea you had entered the room. My, but you know how to scare a person." She spoke on as he noted the way she slid a book overtop her paper in an attempt to subtly conceal from him whatever it was she was doing.

"My apologies, however, you were so focused," he said, reaching out a hand to steady her. "What was it that so captured your attention?"

"Oh, nothing at all, just correspondence to my sister," she said with a wave of her hand.

"Is anything the matter?"

"Of course not, why would you think so?" she looked at him in confusion.

"Because you are hiding your letter from me."

"Oh, not at all," she said with a forced laugh. "I merely thought you might find some of my ramblings to her rather silly."

He raised one eyebrow. "Read me a passage and I shall be the judge of that."

"No, no, you do not have time for that," she said, picking up the papers and books in her arms and making for the door.

He put his hands on her shoulders to stop her and took the books from her.

"I can manage, Alastair," she said, and he could see the flick of panic enter her eyes.

"Do not worry, I will not spirit away your correspondence," he said. "I will simply carry it for you to your chamber."

They walked together in silence until they reached the doorway of her room. "I shall see you in a few hours," he said. "I look forward to the opportunity to be the first to view whatever costume you shall choose for the Duchess of Stowe's ball."

As he left her, he could feel her gaze burning into his back. She was hiding something from him, that was for certain, and he desperately wanted to know what it was. He was unsure why it bothered him to such a great extent, however knowing his wife's penchant for going so far outside of what society expected of her, he knew he had cause to worry.

* * *

ALASTAIR LED Olivia into the Duke and Duchess of Stowe's ballroom with smiles for their hosts. They were a striking couple. Of course, all knew of the Duchess' humble beginnings, but Olivia remarked to Alastair that in her few conversations with the woman, she found her much kinder and more relatable than most of the women of the *ton* with whom she was acquainted.

They had not walked far into the room when a small, slight woman who was nearly overtaken by her ornamented blue dress gracefully began hurrying over to them.

"Oh, Rosalind!" Olivia exclaimed, turning to Alastair with a guilty expression. "It has been far too long since I have seen her. I suppose I have simply been preoccupied."

"Olivia!" her friend greeted her with a broad smile and outstretched hands. "How wonderful to see you, darling. Is this not a beautiful home? I believe this is the first ball here since the Duke held his memorable masquerade."

The two of them began to chatter, as Alastair found women often did with their close acquaintances, and he asked Olivia to save a dance for him later in the evening. "Oh, but you are married now!" said Rosalind, looking somewhat shocked at his suggestion. He laughed. "I enjoy dancing, as does Olivia," he said. "Let the women speak of our scandalous behavior, I care not!" He then made his way through the crowd to find himself a drink and his friends. He spied Lord Merryweather and Lord Penn, but found his path blocked by a young woman he recognized — Lady Hester Montgomery.

"Your Grace," she said, dipping into a low curtsy but keeping her eyes coyly looking up at him through thick lashes, her mouth curled into a smile that looked rather sinister to him, though how that was possible he wasn't sure. She had been trying to capture his attention for years, but he had always found her rather desperate, lacking any significant character or intrigue. The complete opposite of his wife, he realized.

He nodded to her. "Lady Montgomery," he said, and made to continue on his way when she stopped him. "They are beginning a waltz, Your Grace," she said. "Would you care to dance?"

He blinked in surprise. Why on earth would this woman ask him, a married man, to dance with her? It was quite untoward and simply not done for a woman to request a dance. And yet it would be equally rude of him to refuse. He cleared his throat, trying to find some excuse, but nothing rushed to mind. He supposed his drink could wait the length of one dance.

When he nodded, a smile bloomed over her face, and she latched onto his arm as they made their way to the ballroom floor.

* * *

"Rosalind." Olivia's tone caused her friend to whip her head around to determine what had caused Olivia such displeasure. "Please tell me you do not see my husband dancing a *waltz* with Hester Montgomery?"

Rosalind, who was not quite as tall as Olivia, stood on her toes to try to see the dance floor, her eyes sweeping from one side to the other as she looked for the couple.

"I do not believe ... oh yes. Oh, dear. I am sorry, Olivia, but you are correct."

"Why in God's name would he ask such a woman to dance a waltz, particularly when we've only just arrived?"

"Perhaps his hand was forced?"

Olivia's face darkened. "A man — particularly a duke — can choose when and with whom he shall dance."

Rosalind sensed her friend's anger and attempted another tactic. "He did promise a dance with you, later, no matter how untoward that may be. Besides, Olivia, the last time I spoke with you, you told me you cared not what the Duke did with his own time, that this was a forced arrangement you were making do with. Is this no longer the case? Do you now care for him?"

"No, I —" she looked at her friend's knowing face. "Fine. Yes, yes I do care, though I have tried so hard not to. For if I give my heart to such a man, he will likely break it, and I have no wish to live through that."

"You do not know that he would be so careless with your affections," Rosalind said, shaking her head. "You say you are fond of him. I am sure he cares for you as well. Perhaps in time, that could even grow to love, could it not?"

"Doubtful," said Olivia. "Even should he care for me, he still has his desires to satisfy, be they at the gambling tables or ... or elsewhere. I know better than to expect more from a man like that. Though he does allow me my freedom, and for that I am grateful."

"Have you told him of your identity as P.J. Scott?"

"No," said Olivia, shaking her head. "While I now realize he could very well be understanding, since I have taken up correspondence with him as the man, I cannot very well reveal who I am, for then he would know I have been lying all this time."

"Oh, Olivia," sighed Rosalind. "You can be as stubborn as

a mule sometimes. I am sure he would forgive you, perhaps even respect you for your wisdom. Why, when you are in the same room together, the man can hardly keep his eyes from you. And you must know you are rather a vision this evening."

Olivia was rather pleased with her ensemble, a cerulean blue satin gown that showcased her bosom perfectly — just enough but not too much — that hugged her waistline and flowed to the floor. The gold necklace which had been a gift from her mother upon her wedding day still hung around her throat.

When Olivia shook her head to Rosalind's compliment, her friend sighed and led her away to join friends as they kept a close eye on the dance floor.

* * *

OLIVIA COULD HARDLY WAIT to tell her husband what she thought of him and the blasted Lady Hester Montgomery. Her dance with him was approaching, which would give her ample opportunity to tell him so, though no matter where she looked, she could not catch sight of him.

"Have you misplaced anything of importance?" Olivia turned to find Hester's friend, Lady Frances Davenport, at her elbow.

"Nothing at all, Frances," she said with a shrug, as if to show her she was unaffected.

"I do not suppose it is your husband you seek, the notorious Alastair Finchley?"

"The Duke of Breckenridge, you mean?" Olivia asked with a glare at the woman. "He will be along momentarily. He is simply waylaid."

"Is that what you call it now? Come, darling, we know

HE'S A DUKE, BUT I LOVE HIM

that the Duke is not what you would call ... a faithful man." Frances shot her a knowing grin.

Olivia gritted her teeth. "My husband may have had a dalliance or two in the past, but I can assure you that I have no qualms about his faithfulness to me since we have been married."

Frances tsked, "I always thought you were much more intelligent than that, Olivia, dear," she said. "Can you tell me truly that you know where he is, night in and night out? That he never leaves your home in search of another? You must know that he is not the type of man that will be with one woman and only one woman for the rest of his life. He is not that kind of man, though most are not, unfortunately."

"Well," said Olivia, trying to cover the panic that was beginning to form in her stomach. She could not show Frances that her words had any affect, although the silly woman was right. There had been many nights when Olivia had no idea where her husband was, although of late he had been with her or had stayed in residence, as far as she was aware.

As for where he was now....

"If you must know," said Frances with a sigh, as if it were difficult to share with Olivia what she knew. "He and Lady Hester made off with one another following their dance."

"They what?" Olivia whirled around, no longer hiding her emotions as she stared at the woman, who smiled in satisfaction.

"Why, yes, he was quite taken with her, and so she offered to show him the gardens. They have been gone some time, though, I would have thought they'd have returned long ago by now..."

She trailed off as Olivia pushed passed her, down the long corridor which led out of the ballroom to the many rooms beyond. She rushed down the hall, pushing open the doors leading out to the gardens. There was still a chill to the air, and she rubbed her arms to ward off the cold. "Alastair?" she called, seeing nothing but hearing something to her right. She turned the corner, and realized it was giggling she heard. She stopped suddenly when she saw two figures ahead of her. The back of the woman in front of her could be none other than Hester, as she recognized the green of her gown, the black of her hair, and the laugh that continued to trail out of her. She was kneeled on a bench, her head bent over the man beneath her, their intentions all too clear as she could see the man's hands on Hester's waist.

Olivia had always been one to confront adverse situations head on. She was not afraid of her emotions, nor what came of them. She spoke her mind, unconcerned about the judgments of society. Never before, however, had so much been at stake.

As she took in the scene in front of her, she felt a rent in her chest that hurt more than any physical pain ever had. For it was not until this moment she realized the depth of emotion she felt for her husband. As much as she had tried to shield herself, she had let him into her heart, and now ... now with these actions he had completely and utterly torn it apart. She cursed herself. It was her own fault — she had known better. She knew, despite his words, that he would never be able to give himself fully to her, and her alone, and now everything she knew could be possible was coming true.

She muffled a sob with her gloved hand and did what Olivia Jackson, now Olivia Finchley, the Duchess of Breckenridge never, ever did. She ran.

CHAPTER 21

Alastair took a pull of his cigar as he threw down a card. He smiled to himself. He had never been much of a whist player but had certainly come to enjoy it since his marriage. Not that he would ever be nearly as good a player as his wife. After his escape from the atrocious Lady Hester Montgomery, he had found his gentlemen friends in the library, where he was content to while away the time.

"How is life as a wedded man?" asked Lord Greville with a grin.

"As it happens, it is not nearly as abominable as I had assumed it to be," he responded with a shrug. "My wife makes life interesting, to say the least."

"And she is a good woman for having you," said Lord Merryweather, as they good naturedly ribbed him.

"As it happens, I believe I had promised her a dance shortly," he said, taking out his pocket watch. The time had passed much quicker than he had imagined. "It seems I am rather tardy. I shall return in due time, gentlemen."

As he wandered back into the ballroom, he reflected on the fact that, in all actuality, he was looking forward to time with his wife in his arms, even for a dance in public. He was certainly not the man he used to be, though he could not decide whether or not he welcomed that fact.

Standing tall, he looked around the room for Olivia, but saw not a glimpse of her blonde hair, which typically stood above most of the other women. His gaze flicked past Lady Montgomery and one of her friends, who sent a smirk his way. Whatever was that about? Paying it no mind, he found Lady Rosalind Kennedy.

"Lady Kennedy, have you happened upon my wife recently?"

Rosalind turned to him shaking her head.

"Last I knew she was looking for you."

He continued his search around the room, finally coming upon a disheveled Lord Penn.

"I say, Penn, what happened to you?" he asked the normally well-put together man.

"I was in the middle of a set with a woman I am hardly acquainted with when she whisked me off the dance floor and out into the gardens," he said, the flustered look remaining. "Next I knew she had pushed me onto a bench and was kissing me like a high-class courtesan. I cannot quite decide whether I enjoyed it or not."

Alastair raised his eyebrows. "That is an interesting turn of events," he said, "and who was such a woman?"

"Lady Hester Montgomery. Do you know her?"

"I do," he said, his mouth a set line. "In fact, I had the pleasure of a dance with her earlier this evening. She was also present at the moment my fate in marriage was sealed. Consider yourself lucky no one happened upon you or you may now be betrothed to the woman. Perhaps that was her aim. Now, Penn, I am having quite the time locating my wife. Have you seen her?"

"I have not, my apologies," he said.

HE'S A DUKE, BUT I LOVE HIM

Alastair felt a presence at his elbow and turned to find Lady Frances Davenport, a woman with whom he was only slightly acquainted.

"Excuse me, Lady Davenport, but I must locate my wife."

"Oh, yes, Your Grace, that is what I have come to discuss with you." Her cheeks turned a bright pink, and Alastair looked at her expectantly. "She asked me to provide you with a message."

"Yes?" he said impatiently.

"Olivia — your wife — she said she had to leave suddenly and to tell you she had gone home. She was looking for you, but could not locate you anywhere."

He looked at her incredulously. "I was but in the library! For whatever reason could she have left so urgently?"

"I - I am unsure Your Grace," she said, shrinking back away from him. She seemed somewhat of a timid creature, and he wondered at why Olivia would leave a message with a woman who, as far as he could ascertain, she did not particularly enjoy.

"She did look for you, I believe, however she returned to the ballroom, provided me with a message, and left through the front doors. She has not returned since, as far as I am aware." The woman looked up at him expectantly.

"She said nothing else?"

"No, Your Grace."

Alastair had had enough of this woman's half stories and answers that only raised more questions.

"Enough of this," he said with a wave of his hand, sweeping by her and striding for the door. He wasn't sure what this woman was playing at, but now he needed to speak with Olivia.

He called for his carriage, but the footman attending him gaped at him, stammering out the words as Alastair burned a glare at him.

"Y-Your Grace, I am at a loss. Your w-wife took the carriage b-but minutes ago," the man said. "Shh-she said something to the effect that you would be leaving with another guest."

"Oh?" Alastair's eyebrows raised, "and who might that guest be?"

"Shh-she did not provide a name, though I have reason to believe she thought it to be a woman, Your Grace."

Alastair tried not to lose his patience with the man, but he needed answers much quicker than the footman was providing. "And why, pray tell, would you believe that?"

"She said you would be with ... I shan't like to repeat the word she used, Your Grace."

"Go ahead, my ears are not so delicate."

"A — a strumpet, Your Grace. That you would be leaving with a strumpet."

The man's face had reddened, all the way to his ears, as he looked down to the ground in front of him. Alastair took pity on him and sighed.

"Would you find a hackney for me, my good man?"

"Yes, Your Grace, right away."

This would take some time, Alastair knew. Time that would put much space between him and Olivia. He hoped she would be at home awaiting him when he arrived, for he had much to say to her.

* * *

She was gone.

How one woman with so many items could have packed and left with such haste, he was quite unsure. She had not taken everything with her, of course, but a few of her dresses, her comb, her brush, some of the books she had been reading, all of the paper she had been scribbling on — what she would have deemed essential.

"Bloody hell!" he yelled, knocking a candlestick to the floor as he turned suddenly to the door. Thankfully it lost its flame on its fall but it limited the light to the sole candle that bathed the room in very dim light.

What could he have possibly done to cause her to leave, and in such a manner? He had done everything possible for her — provided a welcoming home, allowed her to continue with any activity she wished, and escorted her to all social events she desired — be they respectable or not. He had thought she enjoyed his attentions in bed, despite her initial misgivings of consummating their relationship, and he had forsaken all other women for her.

Whatever could have happened at the ball to change her mind? Or had it been a ploy to escape from there? And where had she gone? His concern over her whereabouts rose as he continued his search, his mind running through all he would say when he found her.

He made his way down to the stable to find Roger, a groom who had been with him for quite some time and whom he trusted implicitly.

"Roger," he called, "have you any idea where my wife went?"

"Yes, Your Grace," the man said, coming around the corner at Alastair's call. "She came round here not long ago and asked for the carriage to be readied. 'Tis an awful late hour, and we were concerned about her, Your Grace, but ... well, she was determined. She told Harry to take her to an address on Queen Street."

Alastair sighed, in both relief and resignation. It was the address of the Duke and Duchess of Carrington, friends to them both. Clearly she would be safe there, but at the same time she had no other reason to leave at this late hour with all of her belongings unless it was that she had, in fact, decided to leave him.

He turned on his heel and marched back toward the house. If this was what she truly wanted, to be free of him, then so be it. His initial worry for her began to slowly dissipate — she was with one of his grooms, a man who had been with them for years. In place of his concern came a low, seeping anger. Anger that she would leave without a word to him. Did he not, at the very least, deserve an explanation? There was one thing he could say about his wife — she was an intelligent woman, that was for sure, and she should have known he would want more than an abandonment without even a word. And what of his mother, his sister? Anne adored Olivia. How could she leave without bidding her farewell?

With anger mounting, he pushed open the door to the house, in dire need of a drink. As he made for his study, his steps faltered when Anne stepped out of the library. "Alastair?" she said softly, and his expression softened, as it always did upon seeing his sister.

"Whatever are you doing awake?" he asked. "Should you not be in bed?"

"I was waiting for you," she said quietly as she opened the door to the library. "Come inside."

He hesitated, not wanting his anger to flow over to her, but followed her in. As she took a seat in one of his large wingback chairs, he went to the sideboard to pour himself a brandy.

"Alastair, Olivia came to speak with me this evening after she arrived home from the Duchess of Stowe's ball."

He turned in surprise to look at her. "Oh? And what, pray tell, did she have to say to you?"

"Simply that she was sorry things did not work out between the two of you. That she loved me and would be sure to visit me soon," she said, an unhappy look in her eyes. "Did you do something Alastair? I thought you to be so in love! She looked extremely upset, though she tried to keep it from showing."

"I did nothing," he said, his frown deepening. "Everything was as it was previously until tonight. I cannot understand why she would leave without a word. And you are a romantic, darling, for she certainly does not love me. And I —"

"You are wrong, and I am not saying that simply because I love the two of you. Some great misunderstanding has happened. You must go after her," his sister said, walking over to him, looking up at him with pleading in her eyes.

"No," he shook his head in refusal, though he did not allow Anne to see the depths of his anger, his hurt over Olivia's betrayal of his love. His love? Where had that come from? He knew he admired her. He respected her spirit, the way she was willing to say whatever she thought, would allow no one to stand in her way when she wanted something. He enjoyed her presence, and had come to think of them as good friends. He had also never felt passion as he did with her. He desired her body more than he ever had any other woman, and appreciated the spirit she brought to his bed.

And now ... now that she was gone, he felt a hole in his chest unlike anything he had ever felt before. He loved her, and she had broken his heart. What a fool he was. He passed a hand over his eyes.

"You should go to bed, Anne," he said.

"But —"

"Go to bed. We'll discuss this in the morning."

She sighed. "Good night then, Alastair. Please think on my words."

"Good night, Anne."

CHAPTER 22

Isabella Hainsworth, Duchess of Carrington, received Olivia in her drawing room at midnight without any qualms, as if she had called in the middle of the afternoon. Despite the fact she had likely been perplexed when her butler had awoken her, she entered the drawing room with grace, a wrapper drawn tight around her.

"Olivia!" she exclaimed, after asking the butler to send in tea. "Whatever is the matter?"

Olivia sat on the edge of the sofa, suddenly realizing she was wringing her hands together and still dressed in a beautiful blue-satin gown. Isabella remarked she was somewhat envious of how becoming the color was on her. Olivia stood as Isabella walked toward her. She crossed the room to meet her and clasped her hands.

"Isabella, I must apologize for coming at this late hour. I simply did not know where else to go. I could not return to my parents and face my mother's judgment, and I could not go to the home of Rosalind and the Kennedys."

"Of course, Olivia, I am glad you felt you could come here. You know you are always welcome," Isabella said, patting her hand and leading her back to the sofa, where she sat next to her. "As it happens, Bradley is seeing to a matter at our country estate, so it is just the two of us." Isabella's wide blue eyes and slight smile were comforting, and Olivia poured out the story to her as Isabella listened to her quietly.

"What did Alastair say when you approached him about what you saw?"

Olivia looked down at her hands. "I was a coward. I did not speak to him but I simply left."

"Without telling anyone that you had decided to leave?"

"I did speak to his sister. I told her only that I was sorry to go but would be sure to visit with her in due time. She's a darling girl, and I could not simply leave without a word."

Isabella nodded with a thoughtful look in her eye.

"You say he was with Hester Montgomery, in plain sight in the gardens?"

"Yes," Olivia wrinkled her nose. "Out of anyone, why did it have to be Hester? How I despise the woman."

"And you are absolutely sure it was Alastair?"

"Of course. He had been dancing with her, and when I could not find him, Frances Davenport told me she had seen the two of them enter the gardens. And there they were. He was seated on a bench, she was leaning over top him. Although..." Olivia paused for a moment, picturing the scene again. "I suppose I never did see his face. But who else would it have been?" She sighed. "This is all my own doing. I knew when I married him who he was, what he would want out of life. I even told him to go ahead and live as he pleased. I simply ... it is only that..." she sniffed as she felt the tears welling in her eyes.

"You did not plan on falling in love with him," Isabella said as a statement, not a question.

"I do not love him!" Olivia said adamantly, though she could feel the lump in her throat. Do not cry, she told herself.

She hated crying. Not because it showed weakness, for she realized there could be strength in a good cry. No, it was rather the *way* in which she cried. Some women cried daintily, with perfectly formed teardrops and silent sniffs. Not Olivia. When she cried, she could not seem to help the sobs that escaped until she gave herself the hiccups. Her nose turned bright red and ran like a river, her eyes became rimmed in bloody redness for the rest of the day, and overall she looked a hideous mess.

However, with Isabella's gentle hand on her arm, the emotions of the day, and the tiredness that overcame her, the tears started to fall, and she could no longer keep them in. She dissolved in a puddle on Isabella's lap, and bless her friend, she simply stroked her back and let her cry.

"Oh, Isabella," she said as the realization came over her in a flood. "You are right. I do love the bastard."

As her tears subsided, Isabella handed her a handkerchief and simply said, "Perhaps it's time we had that cup of tea, is it not?"

Olivia blew her nose, smiled, and agreed.

* * *

After rising late, Olivia joined Isabella for breakfast the following morning, though she found she could hardly eat anything laid before her and instead settled for a cup of tea.

Her friend, however, seemed to have a particularly hearty appetite. Olivia eyed the plate full of sweet pastries and looked up at Isabella's face. Her cheeks were flushed, her hair was even more lustrous than usual, and Olivia realized that she had been so swept up in her problems the previous night that she hadn't regarded her friend as she should have. It had been only a month since she had seen her, but the normally slight Isabella looked more ... ample than usual.

"Isabella," she said slowly, raising an eyebrow at her. "Is there anything you should like to tell me?"

"Oh, no, darling, everything is fine," she said, though her cheeks betrayed her as they flushed an even deeper shade of pink.

"Please, do not hold anything back on my account," said Olivia. "If you have good news to share, I should love to hear it. Trust me, it will help raise me out of my melancholy."

"All right then," said Isabella in a rush as her grin widened. "As you seemed to have guessed, I shall be having a child in but a few months."

"How wonderful!" Olivia exclaimed, truly happy for the woman she had known since childhood. There had been some years while Isabella was living in France that they had been separated for a time, but upon Isabella's return they had slipped back into an easy friendship as if they had never parted. Olivia had been pleased to play a role in Isabella's own love story. She was only now sorry her own had not nearly the happy ending her friend had found, but if anyone deserved love, it was Isabella. "You shall be the perfect mother, Isabella."

"Thank you," Isabella replied as she bit into another pastry. "I shall be traveling to the country shortly in order to remain there until the baby comes. However, I shall not be going anywhere until we have determined what will become of your situation, Olivia. I feel there is more at play here than we may know."

"Not to worry about me," said Olivia, shaking her head. "I shall simply have to determine what actions are best to take next. I suppose I am being silly. Many women simply turn their heads to their husband's indiscretions. Why should I be any different?"

"Because you love your husband," said Isabella matter-offactly. "And it seems to me, from observing the two of you together, he has feelings for you as well. "

Olivia waved a hand in the air as if in dismissal of her words.

"I will have to speak with him eventually, I suppose," she said. "However, I simply could not face him last night. I knew from the very start, from that fateful walk up the stairs to the private box at the Argyll Rooms, that I had to shield my heart from him, but dash it all, he managed to break it anyway." She sighed. "I cannot stay with a man who does not love me in return, Isabella. I simply do not know how I could do so. And yet if I were to leave our marriage, I would bring such scandal to our family."

"You mean to Helen?"

"Yes, to Helen, and to Anne as well," she said. "I suppose I shall have to remain with Alastair until the point when both of our sisters are married, and then I shall determine what next to do. I feel Alastair will provide enough funds for me to live comfortably enough on my own. Oh, Isabella, I never wanted a life like this. I wanted love — shared love between a husband and a wife. I should have followed my instincts at the beginning of this marriage and lived separately from the start. Truly I cannot fault him. I knew what sort of man he was, what he wanted of life, and yet still ... as time went on I thought perhaps there could be something more."

She stared off, her focus across the room on a painting of lilies and sunflowers in a field.

"Do you mind if I stay here a few more days? Until I am able to gather my thoughts and return to Alastair's home?" she asked Isabella.

"Of course," her friend replied, softly. "I still believe you should speak with him and clarify a few things. But until the time you are ready, of course you are always quite welcome here. Now, you may remain in your gloomy state today, but tomorrow would you like to do a bit of shopping? That should help your spirits some."

Olivia smiled at her. "That sounds lovely. I have some errands I must run anyway."

"To a certain *Financial Register*?"

Olivia looked at Isabella in shock. "Why yes, as it happens. How did you know about the place?"

Isabella laughed. "I've known you long enough, Olivia, to know your thoughts and your writing," she replied. "In addition, you left some of your articles out last night in the hall. They must have slipped from your bag or your reticule. I did not mean to snoop, truly I did not, but I recognized your handwriting. I read the column in the latest *Financial Register* this morning before you joined me. It is an excellent piece, Olivia. You should be very proud of your work."

Olivia laughed. "How insightful of you to deduce the mystery. You are correct. We must stop at the office after I have completed my work today. I have a column to submit."

And with that she resolved to spend the day focused on her work, thinking not at all about a blond man with unruly curls, a chiseled chest, and a deep dimple which haunted her thoughts and caused her heart to ache.

* * *

THAT EVENING ALASTAIR went to the worst gentlemen's club he had ever visited. The one where he could find the cheapest drinks, the riskiest gambling, and the most scantily clad women, which would allow him to forget all about the wife who had left him and his heart.

"Penn," he said, greeting his friend, who had agreed to meet him here.

"Breckenridge," he nodded to him in turn. "Does your wife know you're here?"

"When has it mattered what a man's wife thinks of his nighttime outings?" Alastair muttered.

"To many it matters not, but to you of late, it has," Penn replied, question in his eyes.

"Well, no longer," Alastair said, as he called for a brandy. His friend said nothing, sensing his mood.

The serving girl noted his summons from across the room with a wink, and appeared not long afterward, brushing against his arm, her low bodice leaving little to his imagination. She fluttered her eyes up at him as she asked, "Is there anything else you would be needing tonight, sir?" Alastair could hardly look at her as the guilt rolled through his stomach. He felt no desire, but rather disgust in himself. He wanted nothing to do with this woman, out of no fault of her own. Rather, he desired the one woman who refused to be with him — his wife.

"I am fine, thank you," he said to the girl, who turned away with a pout to find another to bestow her attentions on.

"Faro, I think, Penn," he said. Faro was Olivia's least favorite game, because, she said, it was all due to luck, with no skill involved. He walked to the table, laying down his chips on the Jack and the seven. Despite the fact he knew Olivia would never set foot in a gaming hell such as this, nor appear at the faro table, he could not help but look for her over his shoulder. He was too used to having her by his side at the card table, or to looking at her across the green felt, her blue eyes boring into his as she gave him a flirtatious grin.

He tried to concentrate on the game at hand, he truly did. But all he could think, rolling round and round in his brain, was, "Why did she leave?" He had tried to be a better man, the man she subtly encouraged him to be. It was not that she nagged at him, nor asked him to be someone he was not. But rather, she encouraged him to do more with his life, to be a better man than he had been before.

He sighed as the first card thrown was a Jack. One lost bet. The second card? The Queen of Hearts. Of course. Another loss.

Here he was, losing at a gambling hell and no better than his father. This was the man she had wanted nothing to do with. Should he go to her? Should he overcome his pride and beg her to take him back? If only he knew what had been the cause of her leaving, then perhaps he could make the change she wished. As he lost another hand, he pushed away from the table in frustration.

"I'm done for the night, Penn," he said to his friend.

"But we have only just arrived!" said Lord Penn, looking up at him with surprise on his face.

"I know," Alastair nodded, "however it seems tonight luck is not on my side."

He left the hell, entering his carriage, which looked rather out of place in this neighborhood of St. Giles. He thought of his life, where he had come from, what it was like with Olivia, and where he wanted to be tomorrow and all the days to come after that. He wanted — no, needed — her by his side. Perhaps she was concerned about the state of his finances. Thanks to her, his father's gambling debts were nearly paid off. And thanks to P.J. Scott, his investments in the shipping company were starting to show a return that would pay off the creditors coming after him for his father's debts from the horse track. However, Olivia did not know that, and nor had he yet informed his creditors.

He wished he could go back to the days when they were beginning to enjoy one another. When they gambled together, went out to various events, and generally ... had fun. To the time before the theatre, he realized. That was when everything changed, just ever so slightly. Perhaps it was his past. He knew she wasn't exactly pleased about his rakish ways, but there was nothing he could do to change that. He could only change the future. And so he would. He may not have his wife, but he would be the man she had encouraged him to be. A man who took responsibility for his family, who lived an admirable, respectable life. Perhaps, then, in time, she would see who he had become, and return to him.

CHAPTER 23

Despite his mood, the next day dawned beautiful and sunny, and Alastair swung his legs over the side of the bed with a groan. While he hadn't been at the club long, he had drunk enough cheap alcohol to leave him with a fearsome headache. The hour was early still, and Alastair was tempted to shut the curtain and re-enter his bed, but instead he decided to start his day with the resolve he had found on the carriage ride home the previous night.

His mother and sister were breakfasting in the dining room, and were shocked when he entered.

"Alastair!" his mother said, her teacup to her lips. "I do not believe I have seen you rise this early in ages. Did you stay in yesterday evening?"

"I did not," he said, his voice still heavy with sleep. "However I returned home early."

Anne gave him a knowing look, but averted her eyes back down to the eggs in front of her when he glowered at her.

"Will Olivia be returning today?" his mother asked. "I cannot imagine her friend would be so ill as to need her for more than a few days."

Alastair had not brought himself to tell his mother the truth of Olivia's withdrawal from the house, but instead had contrived a story that she had gone to visit an ailing friend. Anne had called him a coward, and perhaps she was right. However, Alastair had always been one to avoid the inevitable, though he was unsure of how long it would be until he had to tell his mother that Olivia had decided to leave of her own accord. His mother had already been through so much, he did not want to trouble her with this situation unless Olivia's removal became permanent.

"I am not sure, Mother," he finally said in response, "though as far as I am aware it will be some time still."

She nodded her head and looked back down at her plate.

"I will be going out later this morning on some business, should either of you care to join me," he said. His mother declined with a shake of her head, but a look of excitement came over Anne's face.

"Oh, I should love to!" She said. "Would you mind if we stopped to see the latest fashions at Abigail's? It has been some time since I visited and now that I am no longer in black I would so love to see the latest."

"The seamstress? I see no reason why not," he said, offering her a smile. Having eaten a piece of toast and finished his cup of coffee, he found he had no appetite for anymore, and told Anne he would send for her when he was prepared to leave. He summoned more coffee to the study, where he sat and took account of his finances and his holdings.

The ledgers had certainly taken a turn for the better. His father's debts at the many gambling establishments through London were nearly paid, and what was left was inconsequential. His investments were beginning to show fruition after just a short while. How the columnist from *The Finan-*

cial Register had known such a thing and why he had provided Alastair such significant information, he knew not, but he would be forever grateful to the man.

Alastair reached down into the mahogany desk and pulled out paper as he took up the quill pen from the desktop. He was unsure what he could do for Mr. P.J. Scott, but if nothing else he must thank him.

His composed letter was nearly complete when his butler appeared at the door.

"Your Grace," he said, inclining his head to Alastair. "There are some men at the door who wish to speak with you. They say it is about an urgent financial matter."

Alastair sighed. It could be none other than creditors calling in his debt. Today of all days, must they come?

"Very well, show them in here," he said, cringing. He would have the money in due time, he knew. He thought of what Olivia had said, to promise to pay installments. He also thought of her insistence that he use her dowry. He truly did not want to be such a man, to use the money of another to pay his father's debts.

"Mr. Rogers and Mr. Johnson," his butler introduced his guests, cutting through his musings. Alastair did not rise, but motioned them to sit in the chairs in front of the desk.

"Your Grace," began the first, though Alastair had trouble concentrating on his words by the way his generous moustache bobbed up and down as he spoke. "We have sent you correspondence regarding the debts you owe, that have come to us for collection. It is time —"

Alastair held a hand up to stop the man.

"You must understand, sir, that these debts were my father's," he said, hating that he was speaking ill of him to others, but realizing he must explain the situation to these men. "I have income that is beginning to come in, but it will be some time before it is fully realized. Can you provide me more time?"

"It has been over six months since you acquired the debt, but much more than that since the debt has been owed," said the second man, not quite as affable as the first. "You have had more than enough time. Your debt is due. Besides that, did you not recently marry the daughter of an earl of means? Surely she came with a pretty dowry that could more than cover what you owe."

"I will not use my wife's money to pay off my father's debts."

"Your wife's money? 'Tis yours now." The man looked at him, perplexed.

"Be that as it may, I shall pay my own debt back without any help," Alastair insisted. He sighed. Olivia had made one point that he should follow through on. "May I pay you installments?"

The man tilted his head, considering his words.

"May I speak with my colleague in the corridor?"

Alastair nodded. When they returned, they agreed to terms of installments, however first required a lump sum to be paid within the week. A sum that Alastair currently did not have, aside from Olivia's dowry. He nodded his head grimly. He would find a way. There was no other choice.

Alastair rang for the butler to show the men out and post the letter he had composed to Mr. Scott, but as he addressed the enveloped he realized he would be passing by the Register's office when he took Anne to the modiste's shop. He tucked it into his pocket, and decided to take it himself.

* * *

As the carriage trundled down the cobbled roads of London, Alastair regarded his sister and decided it had been

HE'S A DUKE, BUT I LOVE HIM

a wise decision to invite her along. Had she not accompanied him, he would be stewing in his own despondency. Instead, she chattered away incessantly about everything and yet nothing in particular. She told him of Lady this and Lord that, and who were supposed to make the best matches throughout the season. Guilt washed over him as he realized how he had neglected her, with first his father's death and then his own hasty marriage. Her first season had been cut rather short due to the former duke's passing, and her return this season had been put on hold due to his mother still being in mourning. Now, however, it was time for him to focus on determining how she could best make a match, and what she wanted of her life.

"Anne, what sort of man are you interested in marrying?" he asked her, noting how her cheeks flushed a deep pink at his question.

"Oh, I'm not entirely sure," she said, suddenly extremely interested in the material of her muslin gown, picking at its threads in her lap. "Whoever you best deem to suit, I suppose, and whoever might be interested in me."

He regarded his sister. She was a pretty thing, her tawny hair pulled away from her face, with eyes a mixture between his own green and a light hazel staring back at him. He had never looked at her as anything other than a child, really, and yet he realized she was likely more ready and interested in marriage than he had ever been.

"Is there a man in particular you have set your sights on?" he asked, raising his eyebrows as he bade her to look at him.

"Perhaps," she said, chewing on her bottom lip, "however, I do not wish to discuss it."

"Why ever not?" he asked. "Mayhap I could arrange an introduction following your return. Do I know the lucky gentleman?"

"You do know him," she said. "But please, Alastair, leave it be. He hardly acknowledges my existence, and I should not like to embarrass myself."

"All right," he said with a shrug. "Should you change your mind, you have only to tell me and I shall see what can be done."

She gave him a small, wistful smile. "Thank you, Alastair."

They made a few stops, at his barrister and his tailor, before traveling onto the modiste Anne so loved on Bond Street.

"I will meet you within shortly," he said to his sister. "I have merely to deliver a note to the office of the Register next door." As she nodded, the carriage came to a slow in front of the nondescript *Financial Register*. Alastair alighted from the carriage and turned to help Anne out.

"I say, Alastair," she said as she poked her head out of the door, "is that not Olivia?"

He turned and saw only a volume of skirts through the front window of the office. He helped Anne down and led her to the front of the office, where they peered through the window.

"It is her! Should we enter and speak to her?" Anne asked, but Alastair answered her with a shake of his head, pulling her away so she wouldn't be seen.

"No, we shall remain out here," he said. "Keep yourself back from the window. I am mightily curious as to what my wife is doing at such an office, if it is her as you say."

Somehow he knew it was. The woman was forever in places and situations where she had no business being involved.

He kept himself and Anne tucked in the shadows of the building. Anne giggled. "Alastair, I feel as though I am involved in espionage!" She said before he shushed her. As he saw Olivia, her friend Isabella in tow, step away from the desk of the man inside, Alastair all but pushed his sister into the nearby dress shop, where he hid behind a mannequin attired in a brilliant arrangement the color of a sunrise.

He looked up to see Anne laughing at him.

"Would it really be so difficult to simply speak with Olivia?" she asked. "Look at yourself Alastair, you are hiding behind a dress in a modiste's shop."

He quelled her into silence with his glare, though a small smile remained on her face. "Take your time in here," he said. "I shall return shortly."

Ensuring Olivia was nowhere to be seen, he entered *The Financial Register*, bidding the man within a good day.

"I have correspondence for the columnist P.J. Scott," he said. "Would you ensure he receives it?"

"Of course, sir," said the rather round man in front of him. "Though it is quite unfortunate timing. The man's secretary was here but moments ago. She shall not likely return until next week."

"His secretary? Are you referring to the blonde woman who was here, accompanied by another woman?"

"She's the one," he answered with a nod. "I've never met the man. He's a peculiar one, though clearly brilliant. He will not leave an address, so I've no method of contacting him directly. He only sends the woman, who returns every week to retrieve any correspondence and his pay, and to submit the column for the following edition. Not that I overly mind. She's a beauty, and a kind one at that."

Alastair processed the man's information as he purchased the latest journal, one he had not yet read. As he did so, he noted two envelopes lying on the man's desk. One, in fact, bore his name. As he looked closer, he realized the handwriting was somewhat familiar, and he took note of it as he returned outside with his journal. He sat on a bench outside the shops as he waited for Anne and turned the pages, soon finding the latest column by P.J. Scott. It was, as always, witty and humorous while offering sound advice and wisdom that was, more or less, common sense spelled out. What was Olivia doing working as the man's secretary when she —

A smile bloomed across his face as a sudden realization washed over him, hitting him like a slap across the cheek. What a fool he had been. No wonder Olivia had been so upset when he pushed away her advice. He had thought her interest one of a woman who wanted only to meddle in his affairs. Instead, she had been offering expertise to help him and had resorted to corresponding in letters under a pseudonym in order to get through to him. He realized now she had tried to disguise her handwriting in her notes to him, but when he now connected his wife with the writer, the samples would be close enough.

He shook his head. Not only had she saved him with her skill at the card tables, but she was also single handedly saving his entire estate from ruin. What had he done in return? Nothing but rebuked her sensible logic.

His wife was P.J. Scott. Imagine that. He shook his head. What a woman. His admiration for her, as much as it had been to begin with, increased sevenfold. The fact was, he had never told her what he thought of her, what he felt for her. Indeed, he had tried to show her with physical loving, but that had not been enough for her. It was no fault but his own that she was gone.

Now, he must make things right. He knew he did not deserve such a woman, but he would spend the rest of his life trying to live up to what she wanted, what she needed in a husband. Knowing she was at his old friend Bradley Hainsworth's London home, he would go to her, and beg for her forgiveness.

"Anne!" he called loudly, running into the modiste's, where women turned to look at him as if he had gone quite mad. His sister looked up at him from where the woman was fitting her. "We'll take whatever it is she wants. Deliver when it's ready," he shouted to the woman. "Come, Anne, we must retrieve my wife!"

CHAPTER 24

"For how long have you been the secretary of Mr. P.J. Scott?"

Olivia and Isabella exited the office of *The Financial Register* together, Isabella's curiosity of her double life apparently stoked by the actual trip to the Register.

"Just short of a year now," Olivia admitted. "I did not necessarily set out for it to become a secret life, but rather I was unsure of how to tell even my closest friends. For it is not a typical pastime for a young woman, that is for certain, and if too many people were to find out — well, it could be the end of P.J. Scott. My greatest wish is for my work to be regarded for itself, not due to who is writing it."

Isabella nodded. "That is understandable. And Alastair has no inkling?"

Olivia gave a short bark of laughter. "None whatsoever. Anytime I even tried to broach the subject of finances with him he would brush it off as the silly, random thoughts of a woman without enough to occupy her time. No, Alastair has no idea. He is, however, a rather avid fan of P.J. Scott, which is how our correspondence began. Perhaps he would respect the work if I told him, but it has been a lie for too long now."

Olivia had informed Isabella about the letters exchanged with Alastair, and how she was able to provide him advice. She did not, however, provide the full detail of Alastair's financial affairs. As close a friend as Isabella was, it was not for Olivia to share.

"And we just delivered your final correspondence to him?"

"Yes," Olivia said, keeping her head high so as not to show the hollow feeling that entered her when she thought of another bond between them broken. "I took the opportunity to tell him some things that I felt he should know, that he would not care for coming from his wife, but would hold in esteem from a man he deemed important enough to confide in. I have also decided that I will no longer write for *The Financial Register*. If I am to return to Alastair's home, despite the fact we will no longer truly be living as husband and wife, it will become too difficult to hide the truth from him, and therefore I am finished with it."

Olivia saw the concern across her friend's face as she seemingly picked up on her hurt, anger, and regret, though Isabella said nothing of it.

"Shall we now join Rosalind for tea?" she asked. "We are to meet at Gunter's within the hour."

"Absolutely," answered Olivia. "I am looking forward to it."

The teashop was in Mayfair, and when they arrived, Isabella instructed her driver to meet them in two hours' time. When they entered through the doorway they found Rosalind was waiting for them in the crowd of the shop, and once they decided on ices and sorbets, they took them outdoors to Berkeley Park across the way. Rosalind and Olivia had not seen one another since the Duchess of Stowe's ball, and she seemed quite concerned over Olivia's disappearance.

"Whatever happened?" she asked, once they were seated on a bench and pleasantries had been exchanged.

Olivia told her what she had seen, what Frances Davenport had told her, and a look of bemusement came over Rosalind. "You say you saw him with Lady Hester Montgomery in the gardens at the beginning of the seventh set?" she asked. "For it was but moments afterward when he came round the ballroom looking for you. I had not seen you in a few minutes, but it cannot have been long after you left."

Olivia shrugged. "I suppose I could have come upon them at the end of their dalliance," she said. "However long the duration, it does not matter. Now, Rosalind, tell us about your viscount. Have you decided when you are to be married?"

Finished with their ices, they rose and began to stroll through the park, their discussions now on wedding preparations and Lord Harold Branson, who Olivia was not fond of, though she would never tell Rosalind for she seemed so enamored with him. They were deep in conversation when a tall shadow came to rest on the grass in front of them.

"What have we here?" came a familiar voice. "Three of the most beautiful women in all of London together in one park?"

"Billy!" Olivia exclaimed, thrilled to see her friend. "How wonderful to see you. Would you care to join us?"

"Please do, Mr. Elliot," added Rosalind, but he gave a shake of his head in regret.

"As much as I would like nothing better than your company, I must be off to meet a friend," he responded. "I am sorry, Olivia, that I did not have the opportunity to converse with you at the Duchess of Stowe's ball the other night. Your husband, however, is becoming quite proficient at his card

HE'S A DUKE, BUT I LOVE HIM

games. We spent some time in the library, where he won a pretty penny off me, until he realized the time had passed to escort you in a dance. I cannot imagine from where he has suddenly become rather gifted in the likes of whist and piquet. Perhaps he has enlisted a mentor."

He winked at her as he twirled his hat in the air. "Good day, ladies," he said, and he turned on his heel and walked out of the park to his waiting carriage, Rosalind staring after him with bright cheeks and a wistful look in her eye that Olivia almost missed, so preoccupied she was with what Billy had said. She soon forgot about Rosalind's stare, however, as Isabella captured her attention.

"Olivia, it seems that Alastair was with Billy the entire night," she said to Olivia. "He must have retired to the library following his dance with Hester, and remained there until he came looking for you and Rosalind saw him."

A sense of relief floated over Olivia as she registered the information. "He was never with Hester," she murmured. "I never saw his face in the gardens, I just assumed it was him." Her face fell, as the relief was soon replaced with a roiling guilt. "How stupid I was. I allowed Hester and Frances to manipulate me into thinking so poorly of Alastair. A few choice words from Frances, a glimpse of Hester in the garden and I came to a conclusion that was entirely false. I *left* Alastair because of it. Oh, blast it all, what have I done?"

She looked at her friends in horror, aghast at her actions and her own stupidity.

"I pride myself on my intellect. I give people advice. I make fun of the silly nitwits of the *ton*. And yet I fell into a trap that should not have fooled even the most gullible of women. Why did I not trust him?"

Isabella placed a hand over hers to stem the words that continued to flow. "Do not be so hard on yourself. The strength of our emotions have the power to overcome all of our rational thought and common sense. The love you feel for him, the fear that he would revert to his previous ways, perhaps the doubt in your relationship with him, all led to your conclusions. You cannot change what has happened, but you can better your future."

Olivia nodded, her fears somewhat alleviated by her friend's gentle tone. "What does it mean, however, that he never came after me? Did it not bother him that I was gone?"

Isabella tilted her head and regarded her without judgment but with her practical advice that Olivia could always rely on. "You left without a word to him. Perhaps he was hurt, or unsure of what sort of reception to expect from you. There is no way to truly know for certain unless you ask him yourself."

Olivia nodded, resolve flooding through her. "I must make things right. I *will* make things right." A sudden thought entered her mind and she looked about for the carriage. "I must return to your house immediately, Isabella. Do you mind awfully, Rosalind? I am sorry for leaving so suddenly."

"Not at all!" her friend replied. "In fact, I insist. Be honest with him, Olivia. Tell him you love him, and then you will know for sure what you wish to do going forward."

Olivia nodded, fear burning through her at the thought of telling Alastair how she felt, only for him to not return her sentiments. Rosalind and Isabella were right, however. They must be forthright and honest with one another if she was to have the marriage she had always wanted.

* * *

RETURNING HOME WITH ANNE, Alastair escorted her into the house and bid good day to his mother. "I shall return shortly," he said. "I am off to visit Olivia."

"Oh, splendid," his mother said. "Please tell her we miss her."

Alastair nodded in response, a lump in his throat. Olivia had brought so much light and brightness to their home. She had become one of their family so quickly, her presence had left a hole that only she could fill.

He was doffing his hat once again when the butler came striding down the corridor to deposit the day's mail in Alastair's study.

"A boy just delivered a letter to you, Your Grace, from *The Financial Register*," the man said. "You had previously asked that I notify you whenever correspondence arrived from the Register."

Alastair had previously been most interested in the financial advice he was receiving; now he was quite pleased that he had been so eager for the letters for an entirely different reason.

He followed the man into his study, and sat back in his wide chair as he found his letter opener and ripped open the seal. A smile spread over his face as he read the contents of the letter, warmth enveloping his heart as his eyes roved over the carefully written words.

She cared for him. She must, if the letter was any indication. Not only that, but now as he read the wit within the wording of the letter, the intellect behind what she said, he was overcome with the brilliance of the woman he had married. He had previously known of her joyful approach to life and her headstrong ways, but there was so much more to the woman that he could have never expected. His thoughts returned to his first days of marriage, how concerned he had been to be trapped into a life with one woman. Now, he realized that this one woman was more than he ever needed, or even truly deserved. Her inner strength shone brighter than anyone — man or woman — he had ever met, and he would be blessed to spend the rest of his life by her side, if he could only convince her to have him once more.

True, his life had changed. He did have to think of her, worry over her thoughts and feelings, but it was more than a fair exchange for what he received in return. He could only hope he could win back her love.

He tucked the letter into the pocket of his jacket, and strode to the door with resolve. He all but ran out the door to his carriage, providing his driver with the address of the Duke and Duchess of Carrington.

CHAPTER 25

Olivia slowly packed the few belongings she had brought with her to Isabella's. She knew she should have immediately returned to Alastair's home — her home — but rather than say the wrong thing as she usually did, she wanted to take the time to plan an explanation and an apology that Alastair would have no choice but to forgive. Her bag packed, she began pacing the room as she gathered her thoughts, before she sat down at the writing desk and scratched out a few notes on the piece of paper before her.

As she struggled to think of the words, she heard a noise at the door, and she bid the maid to enter. "The Duke of Breckenridge here to see you, my lady," came Molly's soft whisper, and Olivia nodded, her hands suddenly clammy with perspiration. He was here. He had finally come, just when she thought perhaps he truly wanted nothing to do with her.

She took the stairs slowly, her heart beating wildly in her chest at the anticipation of seeing Alastair. She had to explain all to him, before he told her he wanted nothing more to do with her. She took a deep breath as she paused outside the drawing room door, reviewing all that she wanted to say. She pushed open the door slowly, and there he was, rising from the sofa to greet her.

Oh, but he was so handsome. Her heart burst just looking at him, the sweep of his golden-touched hair, his strong, aquiline nose and high cheekbones. Her eyes scanned his broad shoulders, the biceps and forearms hidden by his jacket that she knew were strong and sure. How she longed to run to him and feel his arms around her again. But first, she must explain all.

She took a step toward him. "Alastair," she said, as he murmured, "Olivia," in the same moment. She managed a slight smile as he tilted his head and said, "Please, allow me to begin? I have some things to say to you which I should have said long ago."

She hesitated, wanting so badly to speak, but he looked more vulnerable and earnest than she had ever seen him before, and she nodded her acquiescence.

"You asked many times about my affairs and I repeatedly brushed off your questions and your interest. I apologize for that. I received a letter from the man we spoke about, Mr. P.J. Scott from *The Financial Register*. Allow me to read pieces of it to you."

"That is really not necessary --"

"But I insist," he said as he cleared his throat.

Your Grace,

I should like to start by saying that I hope my advice has been of help to you. You may wonder —

"And indeed, wonder I did," he interjected, looking up before continuing.

— why I chose to privately correspond with you regarding my

answers to your questions of investments, and what I felt were the most appropriate and financially responsible selections.

While you do not know me beyond my column, you may be surprised to learn that I know much of you. You are a man of character, a man who sees beyond the typical role placed upon those in society, and allows them the freedom to be who they desire. You have received a reputation for your past, I know, and perhaps one that is warranted.

However, unlike other dandies —

"I should certainly hope that *I* am not considered a dandy." No, that was not what she had meant.

— who are most concerned with appearance above all else, I know your intent. You wished to restore your family name, and you have worked hard to do so, albeit you did so by wisely choosing whom to ask for advice.

This will be our last correspondence. Due to my own circumstances, it is unlikely I shall continue with The Financial Register, —

"What a shame."

— and I will no longer be available to issue you any further consultation.

I wish you the best in the future. Follow your intuition. It shall guide you in the appropriate direction.

Yours truly,

P.J. Scott

"It is unfortunate Mr. Scott will no longer be providing his advice," Alastair said upon finishing the letter. "He truly has a talent and intelligence that should be shared with the world."

"That seems to be true," said Olivia with a nod. "However, sometimes the circumstances of one's life prevent one from following his — or her — passions."

"It should not be so, though, should it?" he asked, looking

up at her. "Anyway, I have written a letter back to Mr. Scott, and I should like to read it to you."

"Please do not feel it necessary," she said. "I know that —"

"You shall want to hear this, I believe. Would you care to sit?"

Olivia walked further into the room, and slowly sunk down before him onto the sofa he had previously occupied.

Alastair began to speak, although Olivia noted he did not refer to any paper in front of him, but rather stared at her, the ocean of his green eyes boring into hers.

"Dear Mr. Scott," he said. "I have enjoyed our correspondence over the past few months. You have been invaluable to me, and I have come to realize just how much so. You offered me advice with no intention other than to assist me, and I brushed much of it aside, as I did not fully realize just how worthwhile, how intelligent, how incredibly remarkable you are. We had fun together, that is for certain. Underlying the adventure of the exciting times we shared, however, I now understand there is a much deeper emotion that remains in my heart.

"The financial solvency of my estate is no longer of the greatest importance to me. Nor are the accumulated debts, many of which you have single handedly managed to absolve me of, with not only your sound advice, but your proficiency at the card table."

Olivia's eyes widened and her mouth dropped as he spoke. He *knew*. He knew she was P.J. Scott. And yet he did not seem to care. In fact it seemed ... he admired her for her work.

"Olivia," he said, dropping to his knees in front of her, his heady scent of sandalwood that she so missed engulfing her as he took her hands in his. "Your absence has left a hole in my home, my bed, and my soul. I took you for granted, saw you as a responsibility in my life. I knew I had come to care for you, but I did not realize the depth of my feelings for you. I love you, Olivia Finchley, with all of my heart. I am such an idiot to have not come to the realization sooner, and I must apologize for whatever I did to push you away from me. Perhaps I was simply acting the fool, but I vow to you those days are gone. Please come home with me, be my wife, and my partner in all things."

Tears formed in her eyes and, for once, Olivia cared naught that she would cry as she sunk down off the sofa to her knees beside him on the floor, her skirts billowing out around them.

"Oh Alastair," she said, finally breaking her silence, "do you truly mean it?"

"I do, with all of my heart," he said. "I can think of no better partner through life than a woman who would prefer to be in breeches at a card table than drinking tea in the finest dress."

She laughed. "I love you too, Alastair. I believe I have from the moment you caught me at Lady Atwood's in disguise and said not a word to anyone else. But you must know, you have nothing to apologize for. It is I who was a fool. I allowed a silly twit of a female to manipulate my emotions to believe you to be a man you no longer are. I promise to never allow another to come between us again, but to trust you and come to you first with all my concerns. If you can forgive me once I explain all to you, then I would love nothing more than return to you as the wife you deserve."

"There is nothing to forgive," he said, resting his forehead against hers. It irked him that she would doubt him, yes, but his relief at having her return to him overcame any other emotion that remained. "The past is behind us now. Come home and let us start a future together."

She nodded against his head, and his lips found hers,

locking onto them with a frenzied passion as all of their pent-up emotions, all of the love they felt for one another came bursting through. Alastair's lips roved over hers again and again, his tongue strong and insistent, and Olivia began to desire him with a wanting unmatched by any she had previously felt. She broke away from his kiss and whispered in his ear. "Alastair," she breathed, "take me home."

He was in full agreement, and with hardly a farewell to the grinning Isabella who met them in the foyer, they were in his carriage with her prepared bags, rushing home.

The short carriage ride seemed interminably long, though it gave Olivia the opportunity to tell Alastair, in detail, how she had come to her misunderstanding of the situation at the Duchess of Stowe's ball. Alastair was silent, and Olivia tapped her foot nervously, fearing all was lost at her doubt of his faithfulness.

"I am sorry, Alastair," she said. "If nothing else," she cracked a smile, "I should have known you smarter than to repeat your lesson of ruining another young woman of the *ton*."

"Although," he said, relieving her fear with the mischievous grin she so loved, the one that showcased the deep dimples of his cheeks, "it seemed to work out for me rather well the last time."

She laughed in relief as he pulled her to him, kissing her cheeks, her neck, and her lips as he whispered to her words of love that soon became rather naughty, turning her cheeks pink as she squirmed in his lap.

Their return home could not come soon enough, though Olivia heard Alastair's groan in her ear as Anne accosted them the moment they walked in the door.

"Olivia, you have returned!" she said, as she came swooping down the hall, not quite running under her mother's stern eye, but walking at as fast a clip as she could manage. "Oh, but I am ever so glad. I was so worried that Alastair had done something unforgivable."

Seeing the look he sent her way, she tilted her head. "Oh, come Alastair, you know you are not exactly a saint. I am so happy Olivia has forgiven you."

"It was not like that at all, actually," said Olivia, increasing the girl's curiosity. "But I am glad to be home."

"Olivia," Alastair's mother came sweeping down the staircase, smiles wreathing her face. "I am so pleased you have returned. How does your friend fare? Is she feeling well?"

"She is fine, thank you," responded Olivia, though she was rather confused at the Dowager Duchess' question. Had she known Isabella was with child? How could she have? Alastair took her arm and captured her attention before she could say anything further.

Alastair cleared his throat. "The dinner hour is approaching. I believe Olivia shall unpack her travel bags and we will join you shortly."

Olivia's maid, who had traveled home with them from Isabella's seated on the top of the carriage with the driver, trailed them up the stairs, with the footman accompanying them with Olivia's bags. He deposited them in her chamber, and Molly stepped into the room to begin unpacking. Alastair stopped the woman with his charming smile.

"Would you mind returning in an hour to help the Duchess with her bags?" he said. "I must speak with her alone first."

The maid nodded and exited the room, leaving the two of them finally, blessedly alone together.

Olivia sent Alastair a wicked grin.

"And what, pray tell, have you to speak to me about for the next hour?"

He sauntered toward her.

"I believe I have said all I needed to," he murmured, his

voice husky. "I do, however, have plans to show you just how much I love you."

She gave out a shriek as he came and picked her up, throwing her over his shoulder before depositing her on the bed. He stood in front of her, shucking off his shirt, and, despite the number of times she had seen his body before, she stared in wonderment at the finely muscled chest and abdomen of the man that was fully and completely hers.

He leaned down, and she practically purred as he began kissing her neck, his lips following fingers that slowly began inching down the bodice of her dress. It was pure wonder, and she closed her eyes to enjoy.

CHAPTER 26

He twitched inside his still-laced breeches as he longed to have her there and then, but he forced himself to take his time, and provide both of them the enjoyment they so deserved after a tortuous time apart.

He kissed her hard, as his fingers found the back of her dress and began to undo the laces keeping her covered. Once he felt the open back, he pushed himself up from her, and deftly slipped her white muslin dress off her shoulders, easing it down her body and throwing it off the bed, where it came to rest in a white cloud on the floor. He then took one slim ankle in his hands, undoing her stockings from her garter, and slowly inching them down her leg, trailing his fingers in a path as he bared the soft skin of her calves. Tackling her petticoats next, he began to become impatient, practically ripping them off. Thanking the heavens she wore no drawers today, he undid her stays, and finally found the body he sought as he rid her of her chemise.

When she was free of the garments after what seemed like hours, he gave her a wolfish grin. "You were amazed by a man who preferred his woman wearing breeches," he said. "I can tell you, it's a hell of a lot easier to pull off your breeches and linen shirt than this array of frippery."

She laughed as well, until she noted the very serious, very determined look that came over his face. His eyes roved over her body, from the blonde hair piled on her head down the soft alabaster skin of her torso. He took in the swell of her generous breasts, the small waist, and the curves of her hips. His gaze traveled all the way down to the tips of her toes, before rising to meet her eyes once again. They were heavy with a passion that matched his own, fueling the flame within him.

"You are exquisite," he breathed. "I am a lucky, lucky man."

"I will ensure you do not forget it, darling," she said with a grin, then, no longer content with simply lying there waiting for him, she sat up and reached out, first teasing her fingers along his lower stomach, then finally untying his laces and freeing him as she looked up into his eyes.

They had shared a bed as husband and wife many times over the weeks they had been married, but nothing could compare to the desire he now felt for her. It was as if he needed to physically show her the love he felt for her, the love he now recognized.

She lightly ran her fingers over his manhood, and he groaned, leaning over and placing his hands behind her on the bed as she grasped him with longer strokes. He knew he would not last long if she continued, and he wanted to make this time different. Reaching up, he took her hands and interlaced her fingers with his own, stretching them out behind her head. He boosted her up on the bed and let his eyes rove down to the swell of her breasts yet again, the pink tips straining up toward him. Still holding her wrists with one hand, his other reached down to tweak her nipple, while his lips found the other side, tasting her with the velvet of his tongue.

She moaned, and he moved reflexively into her, but he stilled himself for the moment, despite the way her hips rolled up toward him instinctively. He let go of her hands as he suckled her other breast between his lips, and her fingers came down to grasp his head as she pitched her body up toward him, practically coming off the bed. He wanted nothing more than to bury himself inside her, as he knew she would be soft, wet, waiting for him. But instead, he reached up to cup both breasts as he slid his lips down her stomach, trailing kisses down her smooth abdomen, circling her navel with his tongue.

He reached her mound, and he found the bud of her center with his thumb, circling it for a moment until replacing it with his tongue. She gasped as he licked at her, tasting the sweetness of her. She whimpered, and he slid a finger inside her silky wet folds. His circling tongue turned more persistent, and she dug her fingers hard into his shoulders. She cried out then, clutching him with her hands and pulling him tightly toward her. His vision seemed to blur as the wanting for her overcame all else, and he rose above her, taking in the red glow of her cheeks and the sheen of her eyes. She lifted up toward him, inviting him in.

He could no longer resist, and as his fingers dug into her backside he sheathed himself inside of her heat. She cried out, and he slid in and out with abandon. She matched him stroke for stroke, and he enjoyed nothing more than seeing the pleasure cross her face, her eyes closed in ecstasy.

"Olivia," he panted, burying his head in her shoulder, "oh Olivia, how I love you."

And with that, he exploded into her, crying out himself as she clutched at him.

Finally, when they both could manage to speak again, she

rested her head on the glow of his chest, and whispered softly, "I love you too, Alastair."

* * *

AN HOUR HAD NEVER PASSED SO SWIFTLY. Alastair had made love to her many times before, but never like this. He had always ensured her enjoyment, her release, but today it was as if he could not get enough of her. Even as they lay together in the afterglow of their lovemaking, he continued to run his hands over her, kneading tension from her shoulders, running his fingers through the long tresses of her hair. It seemed but minutes later when Olivia heard a scratch at the door. "Duchess? Are you ready for me?" came the call.

"Another moment, Molly!" Olivia called, as Alastair slid her back toward him so that she was completely tucked into him, his body curled around hers.

"Only a moment?" he asked as his fingers burned a trail up her stomach and side to cup her breast.

She closed her eyes, enjoying the sensation, but recalled his mother and sister awaiting them downstairs and sighed. As much as she would have reveled in repeating their encounter, she grasped his fingers in hers and turned to face him.

"For now," she said with a smile. "What do you say we go out tonight? To reminisce on our first days together?"

"That sounds splendid," he replied, winking at her as he asked, "Lady Atwood's?"

"I think that would be appropriate," she said. "This time, however, I believe I am content to go as Olivia Finchley, Duchess of Breckenridge. I am a married woman now, accompanied by my husband. It may cause a stir, but I do not believe it shall be overly scandalous."

He nodded but added, "Of course you know how much I

enjoy Olivia Finchley. Although Mrs. Harris is rather delightful, and she is an excellent whist player, I must have you know. I believe I somewhat miss her."

"Perhaps she will make an appearance in your bedroom tonight," Olivia said, looking up at him coyly.

"She can appear all she likes," he replied. "I shall only have one woman in my bed however, and that woman is my wife."

"Oh?" she looked up at him with a pout on her lips. "And what is so special about her?"

"A man cannot look at any other woman when he has found his true love," Alastair responded, his eyes boring into hers in a way that made her heart beat furiously. "A woman who not only puts his interests before hers, but who makes his life more interesting than he ever thought possible."

She smiled. "Would that be a compliment, husband? In my experience, many men do not enjoy 'interesting' women."

"Well, then, it is fortunate you found a man that not only enjoys the interesting, but rejoices in it," he said. "One thing is for certain. Life with you will never be dull, which was what I always feared of marriage. What I have come to learn, however, is that it is not marriage itself that becomes a bore, but rather how incredibly important it is to make the correct choice of the woman you shall spend the rest of your days with. Perhaps you were not my choice at first, my darling wife, but I choose you now, and will forever more."

She smiled at him. "I suppose we unconsciously chose one another the moment we entered that theatre box together," she said.

"That we did," he said with a nod. "I fear this means I must also be grateful to your mother and that hideous woman, Lady Montgomery."

"Ah yes, Hester," Olivia said with a sigh. "One can only hope that one day she shall understand how her actions hurt the lives of others."

She began rising from the bed when he tugged at her fingers.

"There is one other thing of import I wanted to discuss with you. I do hope, now that you are home, you will not discontinue your column for *The Financial Register*."

"Oh," she said, surprised. "I honestly had not given it much thought since I made my decision. I'm not sure, Alastair. A duchess, as a columnist of a financial journal? It hardly seems proper."

"When has propriety ever concerned you?" he asked with raised eyebrows and a hint of laughter at the corner of his lips.

She swatted him. "Since I became a duchess! Well, perhaps since I have had time to reflect on the consequences of my impulsive ways. My actions reflect on you, and Anne, and your mother, and —"

He silenced her with a quick kiss.

"It would be much more shameful for you not to share yourself with the world. Your wit, your intelligence, your skill at seeing beyond what most men see and explaining the larger issues," he said. "In fact, why do you not publish under your own name? I would be proud for everyone to know of what my wife is capable."

She shook her head. "I appreciate your pride in my work, Alastair, truly I do; however my identity would destroy all that I have built up. Men will not listen to women about financial issues. *You* did not for a great deal of time —"

"I apologize for that."

"I understand that, but that does not change the fact that men will not accept my advice as anything worth listening to, and that is if the Register would even continue to publish my work. No, I will have to remain P.J. Scott. However, I do enjoy the writing and so will continue to do so, with your support."

"Absolutely," he said.

"And Alastair, there is one other thing," she said quietly, and he looked at her expectantly. "You must use my dowry to pay the sum you owe by the end of the morrow."

Molly had heard of the creditors' visit from another servant and had told her, but Olivia did not want any of them to be chastised.

"How did you —"

"It matters not how I know, but that I do, and Alastair, you simply must put aside your stubbornness and your pride! If the money were in my name, I would pay it for you. Would you not do the same for me?"

"Yes," he said begrudgingly.

"Very well, then you must do it for yourself. First thing tomorrow morning."

"Fine," he said, "but I shall put every penny back in the fund. Our children can have it."

"Very well," she said with the smile he came to know as the one showing her triumphant pleasure. "I know with your current investments you should not have any issues."

"Not if I listen to my very knowledgeable advisor," he grinned. "Now, shall we allow poor Molly to come in and prepare you for dinner?"

Olivia nodded, watching Alastair as he dressed with warmth in her heart. He nodded to her, a grin on his lips as he stepped through the adjoining door to his own chambers while Olivia donned her chemise and bid Molly to enter.

Olivia sighed in contentment. She had never imagined such a day would come, that she would find a man who desired her for more than her face or her body, but who would know of her longing for more than what the world expected of her and not only keep from judging her, but encourage her to continue her quest to share her knowledge with the world.

And share she would. She knew most women would be more than content in the role of a duchess, but she had always known that would never suit her. To have achieved her own dreams as well as her mother's was something she had never thought possible, and now she was more grateful than she could have ever known.

CHAPTER 27

Olivia had seen Anne excited on many occasions, but never more so than the evening of her return to London's social scene following the death of her father.

It had been a week since Olivia had returned home, and her contentment was now fully realized. She was fortunate to have found a man who craved social events as much as she, and together they found enjoyment in a wide variety of pursuits, from the whist table to the theatre to the balls, to nights alone at home which had become equally as enjoyable. She had been happy before, but now her heart was full with the knowledge of the love she shared with her husband.

She knocked on the door of Anne's room and entered at her call. The girl stood in front of the ornate oval mirror inlaid in gold, staring at herself in the long white silk gown, embroidery climbing up the front to the high waistline and gathered bodice. Olivia approached her from behind, dressed in a lavender gown, the bodice and sleeves decorated with a simple ornamentation, highlighted by a beautiful simple cross of gemstones round her neck from Alastair.

"Anne, you look absolutely beautiful," she said, as she placed her hands on the shoulders of her sister-in-law, who was only slightly shorter than she was.

"As do you," said Anne, turning to Olivia. "What a beautiful color."

"Yes, though not the pristine white of innocence," she replied with a smile. "Now, come, I have something for you."

She passed her a small package, wrapped in white ribbon. Anne looked up at her with a slight smile before her long fingers pried open the package, revealing a diamond comb for her hair. She gasped as she picked it up and held it to the side of her head.

"Oh, Olivia, why it is simply beautiful!" she exclaimed, as Olivia took it from her and placed it into the sandy tresses of her hair, next to the elegant arrangement her maid had finally completed but moments before. "But why ... why for me and not yourself?"

"Because it's a gift, silly," she said with a laugh. "This day is for you, and the diamond reminded me of you — a girl with spirit that shines brighter than any other in the room."

"What of your own sister?"

"I have sent a gift for her as well, a broach of aquamarine jewels that was perfect for her, as this is for you."

"What were your first balls like?

Olivia gave a little laugh. "They were some time ago, to be sure. I said all the wrong things and practically tripped over my own feet, as I have always done. You, on the other hand, have always known how to charm all you meet, just like your brother. Simply be yourself, and all will be quite overcome by you."

Anne beamed at her. "I will do so," she said. "I am happy to have you with me."

Olivia forced back a tear and swallowed the lump in her throat. "Come," she said. "Alastair awaits us."

* * *

As they entered the ballroom, Olivia first found her parents in the crowd. Helen stood awkwardly next to them, and Olivia's heart went out to her sister. True, they had never been particularly close, but she knew that for all that she herself spoke whatever words came to mind, her sister spoke nearly not at all. Her mother had always been exasperated by the two of them, her life's work having been devoted to seeing them married well.

In that regard, thought Olivia with a wry grin, she had halfway succeeded, as Olivia was now married to a man who had, at one point, been one of the most eligible bachelors of the *ton*, one no one had ever thought would settle down.

"Mother, Father," Olivia said to them as Alastair kissed her mother's hand and shook her father's, before she turned to Helen and enveloped her in a large hug. "Helen, darling, you must tell me all that has happened since I left," said Olivia.

"Nothing at all," said Helen. "It has been rather quiet and boring at home since you have been gone."

"I can imagine that," interjected Alastair, before Olivia turned to him with an eyebrow raised.

"Olivia," Helen whispered to her, drawing her close. "How in heaven's name am I supposed to find myself a husband when I can hardly speak to any of these gentlemen?"

"Simply be yourself," Olivia said. "Speak to the men as if they were one of your friends."

"You do not understand how difficult that is for someone like me," said Helen, as she fingered the broach Olivia had given her, which was now pinned to her dress. Olivia realized then how remiss she had been in not properly acknowledging her younger sister over the years they had spent together in their parents' home. She had been much older than Helen, true, but still, she had always been too busy, too uninterested in her sister, who had always trailed along after her.

"What do you enjoy most, Helen?" she asked her.

"Reading," she said. "Dancing, though more so in the privacy of my bedroom."

Olivia smiled. "Look around the room," she said. "Perhaps the men that would be more suited to you are not so much the ones currently on the dance floor, but those on the periphery, as you are."

"Lady Helen," Alastair approached them. "Would you permit me a dance with you? It does not seem fair to hide your beauty away from others in the room."

Helen blushed as Alastair took her hand, propelling her into the center of the ballroom. Olivia spoke with her parents while he did so, finding her mother much more agreeable now that they were on equal footing, and she was not so desperately trying to marry her off. Her father gave her shoulder a quick squeeze of fondness, and Olivia smiled into the eyes that were so like her own, realizing how much she had missed him. She resolved to do better at keeping up visits with them.

"Olivia," her father said quietly into her ear, away from her mother's ears. "I must tell you, my dear, I am extremely proud of you. Not only have you made a good match, which has kept your mother happy, but you have put that intellect of yours to good use and I am well pleased. And more than anything, you seem truly happy, which gladdens me. See that the duke of yours treats you well, daughter."

"I will, Father," she said with a smile at him. "And he will, I know it."

Olivia was happy to watch the whirl of dancers from the side of the dance floor next to her father. She watched as

Alastair finished his dance with Helen, but instead of returning her to her parents, he walked her to the side of the room and introduced her to a comely man who looked near as young as she and likely as nervous, telling by the blush that rose up his cheeks as he bowed low over her hand.

Olivia was pleased when Alastair returned to her, and her father moved off to speak with an acquaintance. Before she could say a word to her husband, however, she spotted Lady Hester Montgomery coming their way and grimaced. "There is the Witch herself," Olivia sighed into Alastair's ear.

Alastair grunted. "There is no need to speak with her. Come," he said, and made to move by the woman without acknowledging her. Olivia was about to follow him, but something about the look in the woman's eye made her stop. Before the hard look passed over her face, first there was something else there — a desperate yearning as she took in the pair of them, and in that instant, Olivia could find nothing but pity for the woman, that she had to stoop as low as she did in an attempt to ruin the happiness of another simply because she had not yet found her own.

"Hester," she said with a nod as the woman came to a stop in front of them. "Lovely to see you."

"Ah, darling Olivia," Hester replied, her face wreathed in a smile that did not quite reach her eyes. "And Your Grace. How wonderful to encounter you this evening."

Alastair never responded, but simply stared the woman down.

"I am happy to see you are well once again. I had heard that you were living with the Duchess of Carrington for a time, Olivia," Hester said, narrowing her eyes at her.

"I did have a lovely stay with Isabella while her husband had returned to his country estate," Olivia replied with a smile, placing one hand on Alastair's chest. "And how I missed my husband during that time and am so happy to be by his side once more. Enjoy your evening, Hester."

She felt the woman's eyes shooting into her back, but Olivia allowed Alastair to lead her away, beyond the dance floor to a quiet space in the corner where they could have a quiet moment alone.

"I cannot abide that woman for more than a moment," Alastair said to her, his teeth gritted as he focused on her.

"Yes, however, if it were not for her, we would not find ourselves as we are today," Olivia reminded him.

"I seem to recall your lovely mother also having a role to play in the beginning of our ... courtship," he said, winking at her.

Olivia sighed. "Yes, she admitted as much. From what I gather, Hester followed us and on the way told Mother what she suspected. Rather than stopping her, Mother was more than pleased to disgrace the both of us. She claims my happiness was worth the family's ruination. I believe more importantly she wanted to have ties to a duke."

"For all that happened, I would do it over and over again," he said. "If for no other reason than to relive my first kiss with you once more."

"Just a kiss?" she asked coyly.

"'Tis all I need," he said, his face mockingly serious. "Though if my wife were willing and wanting, I would gladly provide my services for more."

"Willing and wanting indeed," she laughed. "No more talk of this, in the midst of a respectable ball."

"I shall save my talk until we are home," he promised. "'Tis a pity that now that Mother and Anne have left their mourning behind, we no longer have the carriage to ourselves. No matter. Anne looks quite pleased with herself this evening."

"Doesn't she?" said Olivia. "The two of you are both so captivating, drawing the *ton* to you as flies to honey. Look at the gentlemen circling her. You both have the lovely countenance of your mother, though an additional vivaciousness."

He smiled sadly. "If only you had met my father. My mother always provided us with sunshine, friendliness and joy. She was much happier herself at one point, but my father was miserable enough that he drove it from her. I can see bits of it returning, however. Now, never mind that. I should realize how fortunate I am to have a mother like mine in my life."

"I promise to one day be a good mother to our children," she said suddenly. "To be present, to be happy, and provide them all that they need."

"You will be a wonderful mother," he assured her, his eyes warming as he looked down at her, grasping tightly to him the hand that rested on his arm. "Just as you are the perfect wife."

"The perfect wife — for you," she added, pointing a finger at his chest.

"Now then. You are in the dancing mood this evening, love?" he asked.

"I always am," she said, "perhaps we can dance just once, if for nothing than to allow the skirts of this beautiful dress to flow around me while I am held in my husband's arms."

He stopped and reached down, writing his name at the top of her dance card before stroking a line downward through the rest of the empty spaces. "There," he said. "It seems we are each now entirely booked for the evening. On or off the dance floor, it will be you and you alone."

She laughed. "There is no need to convince me of your loyalty, Alastair," she said. "I am fully aware of your intentions."

He shrugged. "I understand and have nothing to prove. I simply desire the pleasure of your company."

She rested her forehead against his for one brief moment. "That," she said, "you have, now and forever."

"Forever," he repeated. "I like the sound of that."

EPILOGUE

Alastair sat down at the breakfast table, snapping open *The Financial Register* in front of him as he mixed a heaping tablespoon of sugar into his coffee.

"My goodness, darling, but does that not set your teeth on edge?" his wife's voice came floating through the room as she took a seat next to him.

"Lucky for you," he said as he reached for her leg under the table, "I like sweet things."

She laughed and swatted his hand away as she saw her mother-in-law rounding the corner into the dining hall.

"Behave," she murmured.

"Those are not quite the words you chose last night," he quipped, and she laughed in spite of herself.

"The two of you are in good spirits this morning," the Dowager Duchess said as she seated herself across from Olivia.

"Every day is a good day with a beautiful woman by your side, Mother," Alastair replied with a grin. "Now, would the two of you — ah, make that three of you, good morning

Anne — care to know what the esteemed P.J. Scott has to say this fine morning?"

"Of course, not, Alastair," his mother said. "Why would we care to listen to your business matters?"

"You would be amazed, dear Mother, what some women care to listen to," he said, wagging his eyebrows at Olivia, who rolled her eyes at him.

"I overheard Colonel Jeffries say, 'The Scott man has brought a new perspective to the financial world, the likes of which we have not heard before,'" Anne said in a fairly spot-on impression of the man.

"Exactly!" Alastair said. "Now, here we are. We begin with a question from a reader."

Dear Mr. Scott, I should like to know your opinion on partnerships in finances. Is it wise to take on a partner? Are there risks involved? Thank you.

"Interesting," he commented. "The response is as follows:"

To my erstwhile reader,

"Erstwhile, that is an interesting choice of words," he interjected, baiting Olivia, who could not currently respond to his teasing, at least not with his mother and sister present.

Partnerships are an intriguing topic, and one I have most recently become intimately acquainted with.

"Ah, I wonder in what regard?"

At one point in time I likely would have advised against taking on a partner, telling you that the risk involved is not one in which you will see enough reward to make it worthwhile. However, recently I believe I have been proven otherwise.

Partnerships can prove to be rather advantageous. A wise man —

"He sounds rather astute, if truth be told."

— told me that the key, of course, is simply choosing the right partner. Choose the wrong partner, and it can cause much angst

between the two of you, leading to tension and upheaval in the years beyond.

Trust the right partner, however, and it can lead to great reward and advantage, more so than you could ever dream. Together you will need trust, respect, and the goal of looking out for one another's best interests.

You are no longer alone, and must consider the other when making decisions, and be in agreement on the most important of resolutions.

If you do not think you would like to enter into such an agreement, I would advise you stay far from it. If, however, you are interested in seeking such a partnership, remember that the best partner for another may not be the best partner for you.

Find yourself. Hold true to your beliefs, but know you may have to compromise with a partner. Learn from one another, grow together, and you will find what you are searching for.

"'Tis the strangest financial advice I believe I have ever heard," his mother said, bemused.

"Mother, you do not read financial columns, let alone magazines," he said.

"Of course not!" she said, slightly shocked.

"Well, then," he said. "It matters naught what you think. I, however," he stopped to intertwine Olivia's fingers within his, "find the writer brilliant, and the analysis spot on."

Alastair would wait until they were alone to tell Olivia the additional news. From the profits of his investments, he had now completely paid back the money he had used from her dowry to pay his father's debts. He was well and truly clear of all that had plagued him since his father's death. With the creditors and gambling debts paid, he felt such a relief in his chest. His next gamble would be to restore his estate to its former glory. Which he would, he realized, for he had an equal partner at his side, who would be there to help guide him, while loving him all the same.

He longed to take Olivia to the side and pour out his heart to her in this moment, to tell her that any day with her next to him was better than any day without.

For now, however, a look would have to do. His mischievous grin with a wink was a conspiratorial look that shared all the excitement, hope, and love they shared today and had promised one another for all of their days to come.

THE END

* * *

Dear reader,

I so hope you enjoyed reading Olivia and Alistair's story! They are one of my favourite couples. Are you curious about Rosalind's story? Find a sneak peek of her book in the pages just after this, or you can download at Loved by the Viscount. Olivia and Alistair make an appearance in her story, and if you want even more of them, they were both also in Once Upon a Duke's Dream.

If you haven't yet signed up for my newsletter, I would love to have you join! You will receive Unmasking a Duke for free, as well as links to giveaways, sales, new releases, and stories about my coffee addiction, my struggle to keep my plants alive, and how much trouble one loveable wolf-lookalike dog can get into.

www.elliestclair.com/ellies-newsletter

Or you can join my Facebook group, Ellie St. Clair's Ever Afters, and stay in touch daily.

Until next time, happy reading!

* * *

Loved by the Viscount
Happily Ever After Book Five

When forced together, can they overcome all that stands between them to find love?

After being abducted by highwaymen, Lady Rosalind Templeton is shocked to find her saviour is none other than her childhood friend, William, now Viscount Southam. Recently widowed and left destitute, Rosalind was running from the only option presented to her -- marriage to her husband's brutish cousin.

William had been dreading this house party held by his mother, one intended to find him a bride. When his desperate brother pulls a stunt too ludicrous to comprehend, William is horrified to discover the identity of his brother's latest victim, and determines the least he can do is to help her.

Only, William is surprised when he suddenly finds himself falling for a woman he has never particularly noticed before. Their growing attraction, however, is tested by Rosalind's mistrust of men, William's first love, and his mother and brother, who conspire against them. Is love strong enough to vanquish all?

* * *

AN EXCERPT FROM LOVED BY THE VISCOUNT

*R*osalind saw all eyes turn toward her as she entered the drawing room. They were so filled with pity that she did not want, and she longed to run from them all to her bedroom and hide under the covers for the rest of the day. Thankfully she *could* do so, but, alas, not immediately. No, Rosalind did as she always did — what was expected of her. She walked around the guests, thanking them for coming and making the polite conversation she so hated.

She began to make her way over to Olivia when her arm was caught in a tight grasp, and she turned to find Harold's cousin Bart in her face. Oh, how she hated him. She had always felt his lecherous gaze on her, which he made even less attempt to hide now that Harold was gone.

"If you have a moment, Rosalind, I must speak with you — alone," he said, a sinister smile crossing his face and making her shiver.

"Now?" she asked, looking around the room. "Do you not think perhaps we should wait until you have finished entertaining your guests?"

"*Our* guests, my dear," he said with a condescending look. "I think now is best. Come."

Rosalind didn't want to follow him, but she wanted to make a scene even less, and so she decided the least amount of conflict could be found by getting through this conversation as quickly as possible.

Rather than allowing her to enter the room first, Bart brushed past her into the study that had been her husband's. It was dark, the walls a deep navy blue that seemed to cave in on her, and as she sat in the hard, straight-back leather chair in front of the desk, she nervously twisted her hands in her lap while Bart looked down at her, his lips twisted in a malicious grin that reminded her of a hunter who had trapped his prey and meant to toy with it.

"Rosalind," he said with relish as he stood, rounded the desk, and sat on the edge of it just inches from her. She tried to flinch away from his nearness, as her entire body loathed to even be in the same room as him. "I am sorry about my cousin's passing," he said, reaching out a finger to tip her chin up toward him, sending a shudder down her spine.

"Yes, you have said that," she said, jerking her head back.

"There is more, however," he continued, his mouth stretching to show his crooked, uneven teeth, and when he realized just how uncomfortable she was by his presence, he leaned toward her even more. "My cousin, unfortunately, did not see to your settlement."

"My settlement?" she echoed, confused by his words. "You mean to live off of after his passing?"

"Exactly."

"I am unsure of what the issue would be. I know I have money that would have been set aside from my dowry," she said, trying to ignore the increased speed of her heart fluttering in her chest. "I am not sure exactly how much there is, but it should be more than enough. My father was very generous."

"Yes, well, there was money there, but unfortunately, my cousin had a few vices, as you well know, and there is nothing left."

Rosalind's jaw dropped open as she watched him finally push back from the desk and resume his seat behind it.

"That's impossible," she said, trying not to let the sudden panic seep into her voice. "There was always money, for my wardrobe, for the staff, for the house — why, there was even money for the funeral! Besides that, I am entitled, by law mind you, to one-third of the estate's profits, and *that* you cannot—" she stopped as he raised a hand, cutting her off.

"What money remains is tied up with the title," he said, beginning to organize papers on the desk as if their conversation held little importance. "While you were married to my cousin, the estate made nothing, but in actuality lost money. You could receive profits, it's true, but there are none. In fact, I will be repaying debts for many a day. There is nothing left for you."

"But—"

"Fortunately, I have a solution."

She narrowed her eyes. Whatever he had in mind, she knew, would not be agreeable. He stopped shuffling papers and looked at her.

"You shall marry me, and I will provide you with everything you had with my cousin."

He sat back in the leather chair and steepled his fingers in front of him, looking particularly pleased by his own words.

She shot up from her chair, not caring that her shock and disgust was likely evident on her face. "I will never," she ground out. "How could you think that I would even consider such a thing?"

"Now Rosalind," he said, leaning forward. "I know that

you may not particularly care for me, but with time I'm sure we can come to an amiable relationship."

"Not care for you?" she said, her anger flaring, so unlike her except in moments such as this, when all was at stake. "I abhor you! You seduce young girls, you frequent more brothels than Harold did, and you even propositioned me while I was still married to your cousin! I will never marry you. Never."

"I know you may be grieving Harold, and I understand that. Luckily for you, I am a kind man," he chuckled as if he had heard nothing she had said. "I will give you your year of mourning, although primarily to make sure that should you birth any little creatures, we know exactly whose they may be. You will live here with me or in the London house. The choice is yours. But in a year's time, we shall marry and continue with our lives – together."

He raised his eyebrows at her, seemingly satisfied she would fall in line with his plan, and she was well aware of what it might be like to be married to such a man. Harold was bad enough. Bart would be even worse. No, she would not allow it to be.

"Thank you for your offer," she choked the words out. "I am flattered. However, I believe I shall, instead, return to my parents. If you will excuse me."

She strode to the door angrily as she heard him laugh behind her. "Good luck," he said. "I believe you will find your father, however, is already in agreement with me. He seemed quite amenable to the idea."

Rosalind refused to turn and acknowledge his words, though she felt her limbs beginning to shake in fear and uncertainty. His words scared her, for she knew that if Bart had spoken to them, in all likelihood her parents had agreed. They cared for her, true, but they cared more to have seen her married into a good family. Her marriage to Harold was proof enough of that.

She flung open the door, startled to find her parents waiting just down the corridor from the room she had exited. They must have known this conversation was taking place.

"Mother, Father," she said, rushing up to them in a manner she knew her mother would deem unladylike. "Please tell me what he said is not true. What do you know of this?"

Her mother seemed a bit apologetic, but they both seemed resolute. Her father sighed as he looked at her. "Unfortunately, it has recently come to my attention that your late husband squandered away your dowry and left nothing for you. What Templeton — this Templeton — says is correct. Everything else is tied up with the title. It would be best if you marry him as he wishes."

"No," she said, shaking her head in shock. "Have you met the man? He is horrific. I cannot marry him. I *will* not. Can I not come live with you, at least until I determine my next steps?"

"It took some time to find a suitable match for you to begin with," her father said, and Rosalind recognized the tight set to his face that told her he did not want to be argued with. "Your brother will be of age soon and will be in search of a wife. It would be easier for him to not have his widowed sister to look after. Therefore, Rosalind, it would be much simpler were you to simply marry Templeton now. In fact, daughter, I will *not* be questioned on this."

"Father, you cannot be serious!" she said, backing up a step in disbelief. "Harold was bad enough, but at least, for the most part, he simply left me alone for the few months we were married."

"Yes," her mother said, "and that was the problem,

HE'S A DUKE, BUT I LOVE HIM

Rosalind. You did not keep your husband interested enough, and so he went elsewhere, and he died because of it. Your name will now be something of a laughingstock in society and it will be difficult for you to marry again, which you must in order to survive. This time around, you must do better, Rosalind. I raised you to know how to keep a man interested."

Rosalind blinked, hardly believing that her parents could be so cruel. They had never been exactly warm, and yet this was unheard of. Her husband was — quite literally — in the ground for not even an hour, and her parents and Bart were already scheming against her.

She couldn't look at them any longer, and she pushed away from the doorway, hurrying through the corridor to the library, the room that had been her solace these past months. She shut the door behind her and stumbled to the leather chesterfield, which she collapsed down upon.

Unbidden, tears began to form, and she willed them back. She would not cry, she told herself. She had not cried when she heard of her husband's death. She had not cried when she watched through the window as they had buried him in the ground. But now, all of the anger and frustration began to build and came spilling out of her eyes, and she let her head fall into her hands and wept.

She wasn't sure how long she let the tears fall, allowing herself this moment of self-pity, but once her tears began to dry she sniffed loudly, searching for a handkerchief as silence filled the room.

She would not go back out there, she told herself. No. For once in her life, she was going to do what she wanted to do, and that was return to her chamber and speak to no one else for the remainder of this day.

She stood and was wiping at her face with her sleeve when she heard a creak. Her head snapped up, and she looked around the room. "Hello?" She called, feeling a tingle down her back. Suddenly she was aware of a presence in the room and took tentative steps toward the rows of bookshelves. "Is someone there?"

Footsteps finally came hesitantly around the corner, and stepping out from behind one of the shelves was William Elliot, who was now, she had been told, the Viscount of Southam.

She swallowed. Why, out of everyone present at this blasted reception, was it him, standing now in front of her? As children, she had always had a bit of a penchant for him, and she gathered he knew it as well. He had grown into a man who was fine and worthy indeed. He was what she would have wanted in a husband. He was good-looking, yes, but he was also kind, generous, and had a lovely sense of humor. He knew how to make people feel at ease, and gentlemen welcomed him to social outings while women loved to flirt with him. She had always known, however, that he had eyes for no one but Olivia.

Even so, anytime she was in his presence she seemed to stumble over her words, her attraction to him like a fence, obstructing any words that wanted to come out of her mouth. And now here he was, witnessing her blubbering like an idiot.

She simply stood and stared at him for a moment. She opened her mouth to speak, but all she could think of was the fact she must look like a fish, as all words escaped her.

* * *

WILLIAM FELT LIKE SUCH A LOUT. He had come to the library in search of a good brandy, for what Templeton was serving was not worth giving to swine. He had been searching the sideboard when he heard Lady Templeton arrive. He was going to announce himself when he had heard her tears begin, and he had slunk back into the shadows. He had hoped to wait until she left so that she would never know he had been there.

Clearly she had been searching for a moment alone to grieve, and he had unintentionally completely intruded. His legs had become cramped, however, and as he tried to find a new position, he had made enough noise to alert her to his presence. He now stood in front of her like a child caught sticking his fingers in the pudding.

"Lord Southam," she finally said, twining her fingers together in embarrassment as she realized he had witnessed her entire episode on the chesterfield. Her cheeks turned a bright pink, matching her red-rimmed eyes and nose. He winced as he could tell she was clearly not pleased to see him. "What are you—"

"I must apologize," he said hastily. "I came in here in search of good brandy. When you entered, I was going to say something, but then, well..." he didn't know what to say to improve the situation.

"You will certainly not find any good brandy remaining in this house," she said with a sad smile which quickly faded. "I am sorry you had to see that," she added quietly, looking down. The black she wore seemed to dwarf her small frame, and he knew that a woman with her coloring — her dark hair and pale skin — would look much better in pastels or vibrant colors. He hoped, for her sake, it wouldn't be long until she returned to them. A strange sensation had come over him, making him long to take her in his arms and comfort her, to tell her all would be all right. He suppressed the feeling as quickly as it had arisen. She was just made a widow, for goodness sake.

"Not at all," he said softly. "I can understand how you

must miss your husband. I am sorry that you had such a short time together."

"Oh," she said with a bit of a start. "No, it is not that at all. Rather—"

She was interrupted when there came a soft knock at the door.

"Ros, are you in there?"

Olivia must have come looking for her friend, William realized. With a nod from Rosalind — having known her as a girl, he really couldn't think of her as Lady Templeton, he realized — he strode over and opened the door, Olivia spilling in.

"Rosalind, what — oh Billy, what are you doing here?" She looked at him quizzically.

"I am just taking my leave," he said, relieved that Olivia was now here to comfort Rosalind. He certainly wasn't any help and had actually made the entire situation worse. "I must leave at first light, and so should be soon to bed. Goodnight, Olivia, Lady Templeton."

"Rosalind," came the reply, so soft he almost didn't hear it.

"Pardon me?"

"Do not call me Lady Templeton, please," she said, and he didn't know what to make of the bite he heard in her tone. "Call me Rosalind instead."

"All right then, Lady Rosalind," he said, confused, but then who was he to argue with a grieving woman? "Again, my condolences. Farewell."

And with that, he stepped out of the library, away from the distressed lady and the woman he loved, doing his best to remove both of them from his thoughts.

* * *

KEEP READING *LOVED by the Viscount!*

ALSO BY ELLIE ST. CLAIR

Happily Ever After
The Duke She Wished For
Someday Her Duke Will Come
Once Upon a Duke's Dream
He's a Duke, But I Love Him
Loved by the Viscount
Because the Earl Loved Me

Happily Ever After Box Set Books 1-3
Happily Ever After Box Set Books 4-6

Reckless Rogues
The Earls's Secret
The Viscount's Code
Prequel, The Duke's Treasure, available in:
I Like Big Dukes and I Cannot Lie

The Remingtons of the Regency
The Mystery of the Debonair Duke
The Secret of the Dashing Detective
The Clue of the Brilliant Bastard
The Quest of the Reclusive Rogue

The Unconventional Ladies
Lady of Mystery
Lady of Fortune

Lady of Providence
Lady of Charade

The Unconventional Ladies Box Set

To the Time of the Highlanders
A Time to Wed
A Time to Love
A Time to Dream

Thieves of Desire
The Art of Stealing a Duke's Heart
A Jewel for the Taking
A Prize Worth Fighting For
Gambling for the Lost Lord's Love
Romance of a Robbery

Thieves of Desire Box Set

The Bluestocking Scandals
Designs on a Duke
Inventing the Viscount
Discovering the Baron
The Valet Experiment
Writing the Rake
Risking the Detective
A Noble Excavation
A Gentleman of Mystery

The Bluestocking Scandals Box Set: Books 1-4
The Bluestocking Scandals Box Set: Books 5-8

Blooming Brides
A Duke for Daisy
A Marquess for Marigold
An Earl for Iris
A Viscount for Violet

The Blooming Brides Box Set: Books 1-4

The Victorian Highlanders
Duncan's Christmas - (prequel)
Callum's Vow
Finlay's Duty
Adam's Call
Roderick's Purpose
Peggy's Love

The Victorian Highlanders Box Set Books 1-5

Searching Hearts
Duke of Christmas (prequel)
Quest of Honor
Clue of Affection
Hearts of Trust
Hope of Romance
Promise of Redemption

Searching Hearts Box Set (Books 1-5)

Christmas
Christmastide with His Countess
Her Christmas Wish

Merry Misrule
A Match Made at Christmas
A Match Made in Winter

Standalones

Always Your Love
The Stormswept Stowaway
A Touch of Temptation

For a full list of all of Ellie's books, please see www.elliestclair.com/books.

ABOUT THE AUTHOR

Ellie has always loved reading, writing, and history. For many years she has written short stories, non-fiction, and has worked on her true love and passion -- romance novels.

In every era there is the chance for romance, and Ellie enjoys exploring many different time periods, cultures, and geographic locations. No matter when or where, love can always prevail. She has a particular soft spot for the bad boys of history, and loves a strong heroine in her stories.

Ellie and her husband love nothing more than spending time at home with their children and Husky cross. Ellie can typically be found at the lake in the summer, pushing the stroller all year round, and, of course, with her computer in her lap or a book in hand.

She also loves corresponding with readers, so be sure to contact her!

www.elliestclair.com
ellie@elliestclair.com

Printed in Great Britain
by Amazon